Praise for Steven Simmons and
Body Blows

"Whether describing the delights of San Francisco, the more banal and basic attractions of Tulsa or the casual elegance of an L.A. beach community villa, Steven Simmons triumphs . . . Simmons has control over language, descriptive passages, in particular, delight with their meticulous and loving attention to detail. Dialogue, on the other hand, has a gritty, spit-on-the-sidewalk robustness . . . *BODY BLOWS* will return you to the carefree days of the '70s, a magical decade when excess didn't lead to extinction . . . A SPLENDID FIND."

—*San Francisco Chronicle*

"Steven Simmons is a graceful writer with genuine sympathy for middle-class drifters. *BODY BLOWS* . . . achieves a haunting blend of nostalgia and melancholy."

—*The New York Times Book Review*

"You are not likely to read many contemporary novels as good as *BODY BLOWS* . . ."

—*Thom Gunn*

"By turns sinister and deadpan . . . this brilliant first novel is a thriller in the tradition of Jean-Luc Godard's *Pierrot le Fou*."

—*John Ashbery*

"STARTLINGLY GRAPHIC IN SEXUAL DETAIL, *BODY BLOWS* IS A POWERFUL, VISIONARY, AND DRIVING DEBUT . . ."

—*Publishers Weekly*

BODY BLOWS

A Novel by
Steven Simmons

PUBLISHED BY POCKET BOOKS NEW YORK

Lyrics from "Brown Sugar" on page 163 reprinted by permission of ABKCO Music, Inc. Copyright © 1971 by ABKCO Music, Inc. All rights reserved.

POCKET BOOKS, a division of Simon & Schuster, Inc.
1230 Avenue of the Americas, New York, N.Y. 10020

Copyright © 1986 by Steven Simmons
Cover artwork copyright © 1987 Martin Hoffman

Published by arrangement with E. P. Dutton,
a division of New American Library
Library of Congress Catalog Card Number: 85-20683

ISBN: 0-671-63670-7

First Pocket Books printing August 1987

10 9 8 7 6 5 4 3 2 1

POCKET and colophon are registered trademarks
of Simon & Schuster, Inc.

Printed in the U.S.A.

For Ralph

•—•—•—•

Beside
the
Bay

•—•—•—•

5

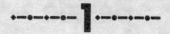

TAKE A SMALL city, for example, San Francisco.

High on one of the city's twin peaks stands a pink stucco apartment house. Constructed in 1949, it contains eight units, two on each of its four floors. From its western, street side the building looks like a tall box, the uniformity of its stucco emphasized, rather than broken, by rows of large, evenly spaced windows. From the east the building is more dramatic. Here the flat planes of its front give way to narrow, cantilevered terraces, behind which you can glimpse sparkling walls of glass. On the rocky, irregular slope below the terraces grow bougainvillea, passion flowers, calla lilies, wild roses, honeysuckle.

I live in the rear apartment of the top floor. Bare white walls. White ceilings. White horizontal blinds against the glass terrace wall. The light is white this morning too, as it filters first through the fog and then through the half-open blinds. Since I've been here I've torn down most of the interior walls to form a single large room, twenty-five by thirty. In one corner are kitchen fixtures, dating from the sixties, and glossy white shelves and counters that I built recently. Nearby stands the room's only furniture, an oval table with a black formica top and two Mies side chairs of chrome and leather. Across the room a large platform, twelve inches high and covered, like the floor, with gray carpet, holds my mattress and a low shelf for stereo, tape deck, television set, video recorder. A brown fur rug that covers the bed during the day now lies at its foot, as do several black leather cushions. To the right of the mattress sit a digital clock, a reading lamp, and a black telephone whose long cord snakes toward but does not quite reach the plug in the wall.

Did I unplug the phone last night before going to sleep, or did it ring in the middle of the night? A paperback, *The Blue Hammer,* lies beside me, face down. Yes, I was in bed reading when Max called. Obviously the phone was connected then, and since I'm lazy, it's doubtful that I got up to pull the plug after I hung up. On the other hand, I have no memory of being awakened or of getting out of bed later. Also, I don't recall dreaming. Normally I'd remember an interrupted dream. Perhaps I didn't dream last night. Oh well. But as I lose interest in the when and the how of the unplugged phone, it hits.

Anxiety, nausea, debilitating wave through the mind and body. Every morning this. Often it's there when I wake up. Sometimes, like today, I get a brief period of grace before it comes. I sit up, reach for a cigarette. My hand clutches air as I realize I quit smoking almost three months ago. No relief in nicotine then. I'll concentrate on a simple object, immerse myself in its thingness, its realness. Sometimes that works. But my eyes light on the goddamned telephone, not that again. Okay, I'll lie back and I'll go through a relaxation exercise. I considered the trancelike state you put yourself into silly when I learned it a couple of years ago in acting class, but lately I've been using the technique more and more frequently.

Picture your body as a riverbed. Hollow. Now let water gradually seep into it. A trickle begins at your head, fills that slowly, picks up speed and volume as it passes into your chest, your arms, abdomen, legs. I see a smallish stream in a country landscape. Dappled sunlight, low leafy greenery on the banks, red dirt, the cool, colorless water rushing around bends and over river rocks. As my body fills, the anxiety doesn't disappear but sinks slowly to the bottom of the water, like sediment.

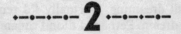

THE FRONT OF the postcard is a Diane Arbus photograph of a small boy holding an American flag and wearing a BOMB HANOI button. The back of the postcard reads:

Dear Cal,

I'm finally coming to California! My agent got me a featured part on "Wayne County"—you'll love the role, a promiscuous, pregnant, alcoholic bitch. We start shooting in LA on the 17th of next month, and I thought I'd fly out a few days early to see you and San Francisco. May I stay with you? Is the 5th, Thursday, okay? I'll give you a call before I leave NY. Can't wait, it's been too long.

All my love,
Karina

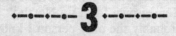

MAX HAS THE largest shoulders on record at the Central YMCA, thirty-seven inches broad. He's toweling himself before a mirror as I come down the stairs to the locker room, and although I've known him for two years, the sheer mass of his naked body is always a fresh shock. He stands six-feet-five, and the record-breaking shoulders are matched by hugely developed pectorals and lats, arms and legs like tree trunks, and a handsome Roman head that's prematurely bald on top and ringed with dark curls. Only the size of Max's cock is average, but, of course, you don't notice that immediately.

"Hey Cal." Max's voice is surprisingly light, ironical.

"How'd it go last night?" I ask, meaning his trick.

"Crazy Bob? Oh, you know." He smiles. Even Max's teeth are enormous. We move to the lockers, Max dresses, I undress.

"So you stayed in last night?"

"Yes."

"You sleep too much."

"And you don't sleep enough."

"Yeah, I know. Speaking of which. I got some great grass last night."

"From Crazy Bob?"

"No. I wish you didn't get so uptight on grass. This is a bitch. Homegrown from up North."

"You're probably the only person I know who still smokes dope."

"Really?"

"You high now?"

"No, just speed. I've got a jurisprudence class at ten."

"Fuck drugs anyway."

"The idea is to fuck *on* drugs. . . . A joke, Cal. . . . So what's wrong with you today?"

"Nothing. The usual."

"The usual? Fear and loathing? All *that* jazz?"

"And Phillip is threatening to quit paying my rent."

"He wouldn't."

"He would."

"Christ . . . you got anything set up for tonight, Cal?"

12

"Nothing definite yet."

"Me either, but I'll give you a call later. Maybe we'll do a brother act. Don't be down. Just sing 'Sweet Virginia.'" And Max leans over to kiss me.

Upstairs in the weight room, there's the usual floating repertory company. The morning crowd varies little from day to day, and I know most of the men by sight, many of them by name, first name only please. The men who arrive in jackets and ties and presumably have "regular" jobs come to the gym at noon and after five, so most of those here now work at night—as waiters, bartenders, security guards—or have vaguely defined "odd" jobs. Others no doubt live on unemployment or SSI, the latter being a form of government subsidy collected by more and more people who are "psychologically" unable to work. Surely Vernon gets SSI. Vernon is the black man with the cornrow hair doing chest pulls in the corner. Vernon always accompanies his workouts with non-stop monologues that are erudite and mostly incomprehensible. Today he's on about the philosophy of history, at least I catch the names of Spengler and Hegel—Georg *Friedrich* Hegel, Vernon says, emphasis on the middle name. But then I hear Aimee *Semple* McPherson, so perhaps it's not the philosophy of history after all. The blond dancer smiles at me as he passes. I assume he's a dancer because of the stretches he does at the bar and because I've seen his powerfully muscled thighs in the shower. Also he wears wool leg warmers, atypical attire here.

More in keeping are the Bobbsey Twins' gym costumes. Their real names are Eric and Jim, but Max rechristened them in honor of their love and their very visible oneness. Both wear blue shorts, white tank tops, red and white Adidases. The cuts of their hair and of their curly beards are identical. Jim sits at the preacher's bench and takes a seventy-pound barbell from Eric. When Jim finishes his set, Eric will take the seventy-pound barbell from Jim. After Jim does his wrist curls, Eric will do his wrist curls. Et cetera. And there's a new face. New to the gym that is, not to me: John Malcolm. He sees me and comes over.

"I didn't know you worked out here."

"Yep," I puff between sit-ups.

"How's it going?"

"Fine." I stop at one hundred. "So where are you working now, John?" Normally you don't ask that question here, it offends people, but John would be offended if you didn't ask. I see him about every six months, and each time John's eager to tell me about some new job.

"Bank of America. Research."

"Something different." Since I've known him, three years now, John has been a graphics designer, a cook in a French tourist restaurant, a bus driver, a counselor in a halfway house for disturbed juveniles, a go-go dancer. Once when I ran into him on the street, he'd just returned from teaching English in Japan, another time he was just back from a "drug rehabilitation center" in Mendocino. Actually I never understood whether John had been giving or receiving treatment in Mendocino, so perhaps that doesn't count. Truly puzzling is how John gets his jobs, since they're all, on the face of it, unrelated, and most would seem to require at least some training. Also puzzling is why John leaves so quickly jobs that he begins so enthusiastically. He never discusses the leave-taking.

"Best job I've ever had. I begin at ten at night and get off at four in the morning. So I have my days free." Clearly John and the Bank of America are still in the initial, enthusiastic stage. "So what's up with you, still doing construction?"

"Yes." The last construction work I did was when I designed and helped build a deck off Phillip's kitchen, and that was seven months ago. But "construction" keeps people at bay.

"You ever think about going back into design, Cal?" I met John shortly after I arrived in San Francisco. We were both draftsmen for a company that designed cardboard containers.

"No, and you?"

"Who knows with me? I never know what I'll end up doing next." No, I suppose you don't, John. But then people who live in glass houses . . .

Seventeen. Nothing. What I'm doing now, John Malcolm, is nothing. Well, I am acting. Trying to act anyway. Also, ass-peddling. And I used to be an architect. Trained to be one anyway. That's three A's. Eighteen. I'm running on the wooden track suspended over the basketball court, and I'm playing a game with myself. I'm on my sixth set of 24 laps. If I can run ten miles, ten sets, 240 laps total, I'll be able to bring off the part. Jean in *Miss Julie*. Nineteen.

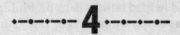

4

Every day at noon I watch *Perry Mason* on TV 20. The plot of today's show turns on a dream. A beautiful woman wakes with memories of alcohol and desire and an image she can't shake, that of a dead man with a gun lying on the floor beside his body. Dreaming here turns out to be continuous with waking: The dead man is the woman's estranged husband; the gun beside his body is later found in her silk evening bag; and, after more plot convolutions, the woman's older brother is arrested and booked for Murder One. His motive: to protect his sister's reputation, which her husband had planned to destroy in a custody battle for the couple's young son Jimmy. The brother hires Perry Mason.

Now the solution to this particular crime lies in the beautiful woman's mind. Perry, with the aid of the trusted Paul Drake, discovers that she is what the writers of the show call a "schizophrenic," that is, she has two distinct personalities. Helen is chaste, soft-spoken, brunette, devoted to Jimmy. Virtuous. Joyce affects a blond wig, smokes cigarettes, drinks alcohol, and is carrying on with a skinny, handsome gangster. Not so virtuous. Further, more eccentric detail: Helen is allergic to fur, while Joyce has a positive passion for wrapping herself in mink. Helen is ignorant of Joyce's existence, except as it seeps, confusingly, into her dreams, but Joyce knows all about Helen and delights in torturing her—for example, leaving her mink coat around to make Helen's eyes water. Aside from Joyce, the only people aware of the split personality are Helen's discreet psychiatrist and her puzzled but loyal housekeeper.

The *Mason* TV stories usually end in a neoclassical chamber of the Los Angeles County Courthouse. Here, in his exemplary way, speaking in a monotone and with considerable dry wit, Perry unravels the always tangled skeins of his cases. In "The Case of the Dreaming Woman" Perry puts Helen on the witness stand and has the discreet psychiatrist "bring out" Joyce. As a hostile Joyce parries Perry's questions, all clues point to her as the murderer. Then, in a typical plot twist, anticipated only by Perry, the true killer jumps to his feet and confesses. Joyce's gangster lover, on finding her alone with her husband—actually, according to the plot logic, alone with Helen's husband—shot the man in a fit of jealous passion. The gangster's confession is gallant and very touching, for he really *is* in love with Joyce and won't let her take the rap for him. Until the trial he's known nothing of Helen's existence. His last, memorable line, "I killed a man for a woman who didn't even exist."

I like the angularity of the *Mason* shows: the sharp-contrast black and white photography, the clean-jawed faces, Della Street's lacquered hair, the fins of Perry's 1958 Cadillac convertible, the tortuous geometry of the plots. The criminal is always found. Found out. Life continues, orderly, stable. The series exhibits a touching faith, as illustrated above, in psychiatry. Also in science, technology, the legal system, and the American way of life. (In one show Perry helped an Eastern European scientist and his family escape from behind the Iron Curtain.) Of course, beneath the smooth surface corruption lurks. In the classical tradition of detective fiction (and of life?), all crimes, although they appear in many by no means simple guises, can be traced to money and/or love. Greed stalks through large corporations, movie sets, campaign headquarters, scientific laboratories, art galleries, "old" family mansions, real estate developments; and scorned lovers are everywhere, everywhere. Oddly, the most frequent villains on the *Mason* shows are corporate executives and artists, especially if the latter are "modern" artists. Are the producers, in singling out these opposites on the social scale, consciously attempting to "democratize" crime? Or are they perhaps unconsciously illustrating their own split personalities?

Dominating, literally towering over the series is Los Angeles. That city of angels. The old granite skyscrapers of downtown loom behind Perry's office window, and guilty parties hurry through chrome and plate-glass revolving doors. Then as now, however, Los Angeles is a combination of the sleepy and the hectic, and the suburban and even the rural are very much a part of the mise-en-scène. Police search for clues in wooded ravines, lovers meet in secluded beach houses, and murderers smile fake smiles on manicured lawns. Linking the parts, creating the whole, are the pervasive, taken-for-granted mobility ("Check that out, Paul") and the sun, the famous sun. Rain falls only as a plot requirement.

Perhaps because of the prominence of the Southern California backdrop, I think of Perry Mason as an icon of the fifties. For I associate cities with decades. Los Angeles is a city of the fifties, as Chicago is a city of the twenties, New York a city of the forties and the seventies. San Francisco? It I associate with the thirties and the sixties, icons Sam Spade and Janis Joplin. I am living, in a sense, in an anachronism.

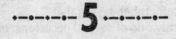

THE EVENING FOG has rolled in from the Bay. Sitting beside the front window in a restaurant called Modernism, we can't see beyond the sidewalk to the street.

"You're being self-destructive." Phillip has waited until after dessert and coffee, but we had to get around to this eventually. Our dinner tonight is the first time we've met in six weeks. That Phillip's characterization is not disinterested does not necessarily make it false.

"Do you need money?" he asks.

"No." Phillip works the muscles in his bony jaw, starts to speak again, hesitates. He drops two lumps of sugar into his Sanka, stirs. I glance out the window, and a tall man on the sidewalk is staring in at me. He wears a lumberman's red-and-black checked jacket and has shaved his head.

"About the rent." The man with the shaved head passes. "Sometimes I feel like an accomplice in what you're doing."

"And what is that?"

"If you had to make enough money to *really* support yourself—"

"I would, but the point is you promised me you'd pay the rent."

"Not indefinitely."

"Specifically you said for at least a year."

"I don't remember saying that."

"To cite only one of several occasions: on the plane, coming back from Key West."

"You know I always drink on planes, you can't expect me—"

"Phillip, it's been a long-standing, unstated agreement. Or rather stated agreement. I can't believe you're trying to make me beg for money. Forget it."

"I'm not, but you know my cash flow problems—"

"You know I hate hearing about business—"

"Since you moved out, I hardly even see you. When you moved out, I thought . . ."

"So you're trying to *buy* some time? Is that what you think you're doing? If that's—"

"No, of course not. Just calm down."

"Let's just get the check." We both self-consciously mime looking for the waiter, but he's nowhere in sight. I study the swirls in the poured-concrete table and listen to the couple next to us. All during dinner they've been playing at seduction.

"Have you read Piaget?" the man asks now. Avidly.

"No," the woman answers. Also avidly.

"You have to. The man's terrific. Really gets behind his stuff." I look into Phillip's pale blue eyes. A slight shift of his head signals that he's also been listening to the couple, and for the first time this evening he gives me his gorgeous, lopsided grin. The waiter appears suddenly, unexpectedly, and places the bill on my side of the table.

"Anne Marie's coming next week," Phillip says. "Do you want to come for dinner that Saturday?" I push the bill across the table. "She likes you, you know." Anne Marie detests me, although during her visit last summer she did her best to cloak this in the guise of solicitude, advice. I was too pale, she said. In fact, weather permitting, I spend a daily hour or two working on a tan. "Yes, the surface tan is there, but beneath that is pallor." I should move to New York if I was serious about a "theatrical career," she said; and leave Phillip. I should learn to cook, she said; if I was going to live with Phillip, I might as well make myself useful.

"No."

"No Anne Marie doesn't like you? Or no you don't want to come for dinner?"

"No Anne Marie doesn't like me and no I don't want to come for dinner."

"She wanted me to invite you, you know."

"The cunt." Again Phillip flashes his gorgeous, lopsided grin.

"Shouldn't talk that way about my mother."

"My friend Karina's coming that weekend anyway."

"The famous Karina. You always promised you'd introduce us. So you can both come to dinner." Phillip takes out his wallet and check book. He puts an American Express card on the bill tray and asks the waiter for a pen.

When Phillip hands me a check, it's for only one month's rent, not the usual three.

"Sorry, but like I said, my cash flow. We need to talk some more about this in any case." And the man at the next table signals the waiter to pour his lady another glass of Moët et Chandon Brut.

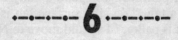

JUST BEFORE MIDNIGHT, a cheap waterfront hotel, San Francisco, 1934. We've turned off the lights, but a neon sign outside the window flickers rhythmically through the thin shade, casting red, then yellow, then green shadows across the room. Bessie Smith moans softly from the radio, a foghorn sounds in the distance. I lie naked on the bed and nearby stands the sailor with the strawberry blond hair, wearing a jock strap and a U.S. Navy cap. It's time, he suggests, to tell each other some stories. All right. The sailor will begin.

He has two shipmates who are his special buddies, Mario, a brawny Italian, and a tall blond whom the sailor calls the Swede. On shore leave the three men often prowl the streets together, drinking, brawling, looking for women. One night, dead drunk and unable to find any whores who suited them, they ended up in a cheap hotel room, fell into bed together. The big men moved restlessly against one another on the narrow bed; it was impossible for them not to be aware of each other's bodies beneath their thin navy whites. Gradually their random movements became deliberate caresses. A thigh moved up against a buttock, an arm stroked a back, a shoulder grazed a chest. The caresses turned harsh, passionate, fully conscious. Hands grabbed at muscles, pulled at clothes, undid buttons. The sailor with the strawberry blond hair moved his mouth to the Swede's. Mario turned his head away when the Swede tried to kiss him, but he, like the others, had a hard-on when he shucked his clothes. The three naked bodies pushed against one another, indiscriminately at first. Then they pulled back, slowly regrouped to try various combinations of mouths, cocks, assholes. Their orgasms came as the sailor with the strawberry blond hair sucked off the Swede, took the Italian up the ass, and gave himself a hand job.

The sailor fondles his cock, now erect beneath his

jock strap. I tell him to take away his hand and he does. He asks if I want to hear about the time he and Mario and the Swede were arrested for starting a bar brawl and thrown in a cell with a group of reefer-smoking hoodlums. Sure, I say, and the sailor tells another story, one of rape and exquisite torture.

Now it's my turn.

A couple of weeks ago Eric, one of my fellow workers on the bridge, invited me home for dinner. Eric's wife Monica greeted us at the door of their apartment on Leavenworth, and she turned out to be a smaller, feminine version of her husband, both fresh from Minnesota, with cornsilk hair, blue eyes, supple farm bodies. Monica's incredible prettiness and her clean, rosy skin made me aware of my sweat and grime, the sweat and grime that come from eight hours of hauling steel, and I apologized for not having had time to wash up after work. Smiling mysteriously, Monica said that Eric and I could both shower while she finished preparing supper, if we'd make it quick. I went first, luxuriating in the warm water and the lilac-scented soap. When I shut off the tap and pulled back the pink plastic curtain Eric was standing there in his shorts. He gave my body the once-over and said that Monica wanted us to hurry. I'd seen Eric shirtless at work, of course, but as he dropped his shorts to step into the shower, I had my first, tantalizing glimpse of him completely stripped. He had a big, reddish cock, surrounded by thick, shaggy hair that grew all the way up to his navel, a startling contrast to his pale, hairless upper torso. Moving past each other in the tiny, steam-filled bathroom, we touched briefly.

The three of us ate chicken casserole and drank two bottles of cheap red wine. After dessert, vanilla ice

cream and fig newtons, we opened a third bottle.
When Eric left to use the bathroom, Monica smiled at
me, I smiled back. She came around the table and
planted herself in my lap, thrusting her big tits against
my chest, her tongue into my mouth. What the hell, I
moved a hand under her dress, pulled down her
panties, and stuck two fingers up her cunt. When Eric
returned to the room, I frantically tried to pull myself
away from his wife, but she held on tight. Eric just
stood at the door staring for what seemed like forever.
Then he came over and, as he grinned down at me,
slowly began unbuttoning Monica's blouse. Christ.
When he'd freed her tits, Eric guided an erect nipple
to my mouth and took the other between his lips. I felt
his hand close on my wrist as he guided my fingers
deeper into his wife.

The sailor frowns, he doesn't like the prominent
role Monica plays in my story. But I continue describing my session with Eric and Monica in graphic
heterosexual detail, teasing him. Eric and I never laid
a hand on each other that night, except to facilitate
Monica's pleasure, and the evening ended with us
both fucking her at the same time, Eric fore, me aft.

The sailor yawns, he's lost his erection. Now I'll
give him what he wants.

The next day, just before sunset, Eric and I stood on
a scaffold, high up near one of the big bridge's
half-finished arches. We hadn't talked yet about the
night before, and when the rest of the crew went
down, we lingered there, both knowing we had some
unfinished business to settle. I spoke first, telling Eric
that I was sorry about what happened if—He interrupted, there was no need to be sorry, both he and
Monica had a terrific time. But when I looked into

Eric's face I saw, if not regret exactly, a puzzling hesitancy, as though he had a question he couldn't bring himself to ask. Suddenly, he put his arm around my waist, pressed his body to mine, and I understood. Understood that last night had been a setup, but that what Eric had wanted, even if he hadn't fully realized it then, was for me to fuck not Monica, but him. I roughly pushed him away. He started apologizing, but I told him to shut the fuck up. I unzipped my pants, pulled out my cock, signaled him to get down on it. Eric fell to his knees, and his sucking soon got me completely hard. I pulled him up, pressed my mouth to his. We kissed for a long time and held each other's bodies against the chill ocean air. I turned Eric around, positioned him against the scaffold railing, pulled his pants down around his ankles. As I entered him, he cried out, but I kept pushing. And there on the Golden Gate Bridge, hundreds of feet above the water, I watched the sun set over the ocean in the west and the lights come on all over the city in the east as I fucked Eric.

"Yeah man," says the sailor with the strawberry blond hair. "Now."

I tell him to lie down and he stretches out across the floor. I rise from the bed, stand above him, try to look as mean as I can.

"Please wear your hat." I put on the orange hardhat and pick up a bottle of beer from the bedside table. I take a swig of beer, slosh it around in my mouth, spit it across the sailor's stomach and jock strap.

"Yeah."

I spit again, this time saliva, and the rivulet runs from his nipple down his chest. I kneel down, stick a popper under his nose, and, as he takes my cock into his mouth, the sailor's face shines in ecstasy.

1978. Now wearing a tweed sports jacket and corduroy slacks, he puts the sailor cap and the orange hardhat back into his gym bag. Our personas were his idea, the place, the step back in time, mine. As we shake hands at my front door, he says he had a good time, he'd like to see me again, and I say I'd like that too. I unplug the light with the colored gelatin filters and return it to the closet. I slip disc two of the collected Bessie Smith back into its jacket. I pick up two fifty-dollar bills the man with the strawberry blond hair has left on the table.

AS WE CRUISED by Angel Island, the loud recorded voice told us that "thousands of the Orientals who later built our railroads" were interned there when they first arrived in America. As we passed the Maritime Museum, the voice drew our attention to an ancient submarine docked there and told us the number of enemy ships—six—the USS *Pampanito* sank during World War II. And now the voice explains that Fort Mason, the group of gray buildings to our left, was, between 1941 and 1945, the main conduit for men and supplies headed for the Pacific Combat Zone.

"A somewhat tactless tape," I whisper to Karina, "considering most of their customers." Karina looks around, nods.

"You have a point." When I met her at the airport yesterday, Karina said that she wanted to do all the tourist places. So, on a cold and overcast afternoon, we're on a boat in the middle of the bay with fifty or so other sightseers, at least three-quarters of whom are Japanese. "I wonder what they think?" Karina says. I shrug. "Maybe they don't understand English," she says.

"My God," a man near us on the foredeck exclaims, "I never knew it was Deco!" The man, not Japanese, has a high-pitched voice with a Massachusetts accent and refers, of course, to the Golden Gate Bridge. It looms straight before us, the tops of its enormous, rust-colored towers shrouded this afternoon in fog. The recorded voice gives a history of the bridge's construction, and the dramatic, movie-theme music backing it reaches a violin-tinged crescendo just as we pass beneath the bridge's central span.

A man appears on deck with a cardboard box containing three Bloody Marys and heads toward us. He hands one drink to the guy with the Massachusetts accent next to me and another drink to a second companion, and he tells them he heard in the bar that a woman just jumped off the Golden Gate. The man points toward the San Francisco shore near which, sure enough, two Coast Guard boats cruise and a helicopter hovers. I look into the deep green water and imagine being crushed to death there by tons of icy water. Karina, perhaps thinking along similar lines, shivers and snuggles closer to me. Her soft hair smells of lemon and honey. The third man in the group next to us, who, unlike his friends, doesn't have a Massachusetts accent and so, perhaps, is a local, discounts the story, says that people don't jump off the Golden Gate anymore.

"There are television cameras all along the sides of the bridge," he explains, "constantly monitored. If you get too near the edge, someone rushes out and grabs you. You couldn't kill yourself from there, even if you wanted to. That's all a myth, Larry. People can't jump off the bridge anymore."

Apparently people can. Four hours later Karina and I watch Coast Guard men on the afternoon news carry ashore a plastic-wrapped body, presumably that of the woman we heard about earlier. Then, in an institutional-looking corridor, that of a morgue, perhaps, or of a police station, a live-at-five reporter shoves a microphone into the face of a middle-aged man identified as the drowned woman's husband. The understandably distraught man says that he can't think of any reason why his wife would commit suicide.

"Nothing at all?" the reporter persists, and finally the man tearfully admits that his wife had been "somewhat depressed" recently over the death of their German Shepherd.

"That reporter should be tarred and feathered,"

Karina says, affecting a Southern drawl. She turns off the set. "And run out of town on a rail."

We each do a line of coke before going to the movies. At a recently restored art moderne theater we watch a rare print of the 1931 *Private Lives* starring Norma Shearer, but on screen Noel Coward's witticisms come across as forced, and the acting's lousy. I lean back and study the gold-leafed pattern of intersecting chevrons in the ceiling. The small amount of cocaine can't overcome the effect of all the wine I drank at dinner, and I drift off.

"Refreshed?" Karina teases when she nudges me at the movie's end. No. Images from a dream linger, a green linoleum floor, a billowing lace curtain, a man without an arm, a mink coat smeared with grease.

I watch Karina from the bed. She's changed into her blue flannel nightgown and stands looking out the terrace window. Her thick dark hair, her pale skin, her violet eyes, the voluptuous curves of her body sometimes remind me of the young Elizabeth Taylor.

"I think I understand," she says without turning around, "what you said in your letter about the light."

"What? I don't remember."

"You said you lived here because you like the light. And the views. Vistas. Is that the word?"

"That's true," I say to her back.

"Is it?"

"Is it what?"

"Isn't there any other reason you live here?" Karina turns to face me.

"No." She comes to bed, switches off the light.

"The lights of the city out there," she says, "they're

30

flickering. They remind me of fireflies. Did you ever catch fireflies when you were a kid?"

"Sure. We called them lightning bugs."

"Did you keep them in jars?"

"Yes."

"We called them fireflies, or little stars. I think I really believed that they were little stars. All of us kids in the neighborhood would catch fireflies in the summer—that was before my parents got divorced—and we'd play hide-and-seek and a game where we rolled around in the wet grass. There was one little boy I especially liked to roll around with. I can't even remember his name now, but at the time he was everything to me. It was always terrible when my parents called out to say that I had to come in, it was getting late, partially because I didn't want to have to stop rolling with that boy. But I had a bookcase headboard and I'd set my jar of fireflies there. After Mommy turned off the light, I'd lie in bed looking at that jar and think everything was okay, the stars were in there with me and maybe I'd see the boy the next night. I realized even then how much I wanted to hold his little brown body." Karina laughs, rests her head on my shoulder.

"He was black?"

"No, just suntanned." As she nuzzles my chest, I kiss her soft, scented hair. Then she turns away and we settle into sleep, curled up like fetuses, back to back.

8

YOU'RE MOVING LIKE a goddamn actor, Kline yells. Well, I thought that was what I was supposed to be, a goddamn actor. It's true I've changed my walk tonight. Ramrod straight back, chest further out than usual, head higher, crotch prominent, legs apart and somewhat stiff. I move slowly, trying to capture something between a panther's wary, sensual grace and a military man's erect bearing. Jean's an animal, a sexual stud, but a very deliberate, very calculating, very controlling stud. He's also a servant, and servants in livery seem to have a somewhat military stance, at least the servants I've seen in movies and the doormen I've seen at apartment houses. I will wear livery during part of the play, and, besides, Jean *has* been in the army.

Stop moving like a goddamn marionette, Kline tells me. My attempts at characterization may be crude at this point, but I have to start somewhere. Of course, I should have known that Kline would object. He rails against working from the "outside in," and hasn't he told me often enough to concentrate on breaking down my "armor"? That my character is encased in armor, has to be to survive, doesn't seem to register with Kline, who wants his actors to show "vulnerability." Jean should wear his heart on his sleeve only occasionally, when I talk about spying on Julie in the garden or when I tell her my dreams for the hotel, but Kline wants to see vulnerability constantly. And guts. "Give me your guts" and its variants are, indeed, his favorite directions. "Jesus Christ," Linda whispered one night after he told her he wanted to see some guts, "you'd think he could wait until I chop up the bird."

Linda's exasperation and her humor were both uncharacteristic. Usually she and Cheryl, who plays Kristin, just nod at Kline when he yells at them and either try to give him what he wants or pretend to give him what he wants while continuing to do what they want, often I can't tell which. Probably the former, since they've both worked with him several times before and seem to trust and even admire the man. Who am I to tell them that their trust and admiration are misplaced, unwarranted? I've never seen any of his productions, I seldom go to plays, but among both actors and the local press Kline's considered a veritable wunderkind. Even Karina was impressed when I told her I was working with him, because Kline's the "discovery," the handpicked alter ego, of a famous Sonoma playwright and has directed several of that hotshot's off-off-Broadway successes.

Be that as it may, I'll take directors who are less primitive, ones who talk instead of yell. I've already learned that it's pointless to argue reasonably with Kline or even to yell back at him. When I've tried to explain my interpretation, tried to make him understand why I'm doing what I'm doing, he's always grunted contemptuously and told me to just get rid of all that "goddamn intellectual bullshit."

Obviously my distaste for Kline's methods has a lot to do with his treatment of me. From the start of rehearsals he's made it clear that he considers me the weak link in the production. Several times he's muttered darkly about my "lack of experience." Presumably he means my lack of experience working with him. In any case, not a phrase to build an actor's confidence, but then no doubt part of Kline's method is to destroy my confidence so he can get at my guts and vulnerability. A familiar director's trick. Okay, I've decided to play along with Kline as much as I can during rehearsals, then on opening night I'll do *my* version of Jean. But right now I need to experiment with this walk, see how it works.

Goddammit, he shouts so loudly that Linda drops her line. The shout is clearly directed at me. I turn and stare at Kline. He sits only a few feet from where we're standing—another irritating trick, why can't he sit further back, like other directors?—and he returns my stare, challenging me. What does Kline know about being a stud anyway? With that greasy black hair, that sallow, pockmarked face, that undernourished body, that orange and green paisley scarf around his neck—Kline's one gesture toward sartorial distinction—how could he get anyone into bed? Cheryl told me that Kline and Linda used to be lovers, but she probably slept with him to get a part. Well, I suppose I might sleep with Kline to get a part, if it came to that, but no. No, that's too disgusting, even for me. His deep-set eyes hold me though. He does get to me, he has power, I'll give Kline that.

Where the power comes from I don't know, certainly not just from his official role as director. I hate Kline, I hate his power, wherever it comes from, I hate his vulgarity, his ugliness, his poverty, his pretensions, his manipulations, but I can't force myself to look away. Our eyes are still locked when he says, softly, All right now, Cal? All right. I drop my shoulders, slip into my usual slouch, then turn back to Linda and say my line.

No, Kline interrupts, he wants us to start from the beginning of the scene, when Julie enters. Linda gives me a look. She's pissed that she has to repeat a bit of business that's physically and emotionally draining, and she blames me, not Kline. She smiles fakely as she pauses and says, sotto voce, You did look pretty silly trying to be macho. The bitch. The pert-nosed, all-American, talentless bitch. Ex-mistress, fuckee, cock-sucker of Kline the Swine.

"I am ready now," she says as Julie, still smiling her fake smile.

"Ssh! Kristin is awake!" I grab Linda's arm savagely.

"Does she suspect anything?" Linda wrenches her arm free.

"Not a thing!" I grab the bitch again. "She knows nothing! Lord in heaven—how you look!" I speak with genuine contempt, disgust. Disgust with Linda, with Kline, separately, together, with myself. What am I doing with these people in this dank basement masquerading as a theater?

"Look? Why—what's the matter?"

"Your face is livid! You look like a corpse . . . and if you'll pardon me, your face is not clean!" Yes, your perky little mug represents all the shit in this world.

Life is a shit sandwich and every day you take a bigger bite.

"Good," Kline grunts, "that's what I want, guts." In spite of myself, I'm pleased.

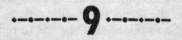

HARD-ON HARDHAT. 20, 5'9", 150 LBS. BL. HR, GR. EYES, MUSCULAR, HUNG BIG, VERSA-TILE. LET A HORNY CONSTRUCTION WORKER FULFILL YOUR FANTASIES. TWOSOMES AVAILABLE. CALL MICK. (415) 286-7431.

To HAVE THE entire ad appear in capital letters is more expensive but worth it. I fill in the dollar amount and my Master Charge number. As usual, I've waited until the night before the deadline to send in the form. I'm drunk, Max and I had several schnapps and beers at the Midnight Sun after seeing Billy, I have a low tolerance for alcohol anyway, and I'll probably regret the construction worker bit when the paper comes out. But you've got to set yourself apart from the competition somehow, and *hard-on hardhat* seems pretty catchy. As Max says, when the economy gets bad, more people start hustling, and last month the Northern California ads took up three full pages. The economy is very bad. Not for me especially, most of my clients are repeats and referrals, business is steady, but I keep the ad, want to make as much money as I can, who knows when Phillip will make good on his threat to quit paying my rent. Besides, just now the evening rehearsals are forcing me to turn down lots of tricks.

The advertisement's idiotic language never bothers me as I compose it. It's when I get the new issue and see the words and numbers in cold print that I always wince. Unfortunately, I have to check to make sure that I've made the deadline and that they've got the correct phone number. I'm afraid they'll misprint my number one day, and I have visions of some litigious respectable citizen getting calls in the middle of the night asking him to perform unspeakable acts. But seeing myself described crudely and a little falsely in black ink on pink paper is always unsettling. Blood rushes to my head, I'm momentarily thrown off balance. It's like catching a glimpse of a vaguely attractive but also vaguely repellent stranger in a store window, and then realizing, with a sickening glide of emotion, that the stranger, this man Mick, is you.

I call myself Mick, I suppose, to separate hustling from the rest of my life. Also, I figure if I ever did make it as an actor the false name would make it more difficult for anyone to delve into my checkered past. That vague, hypothetical future is also why I turn down the offers to do porno that fairly frequently come my way. Max says I'm being both paranoid and naïve; he uses his real name with johns and has done a couple of fuck films. As for the other lie—apart from the one about being a construction worker, which no one's expected to believe anyway—I'm twenty-six but can pass for twenty, at least for a twenty-year-old who's been around, and most johns seem to like us young unless they want a daddy type, which in any case I'm not. The rest of the ad is true enough.

Max is the second member of the twosome. Working as a team is much more lucrative than working as singles, we both double our rates. Max and I met performing as a twosome in fact, at Billy's, the same Billy we saw tonight. I'd tricked with Billy once before when he called and asked if I'd be interested in coming over and doing a number with another guy. I was wary, but the previous time with Billy had been easy, no problems, and I needed the money badly. Besides, I thought the other hustler might turn out to be attractive and we could have some fun. Max did turn out to be attractive and we did have some fun. What Billy wanted from us that night, and what Max and I have repeated for him once a month for the past two years—minus a six-month hiatus when I lived with Phillip—was for us to recreate a photograph he'd clipped from a porn magazine. The fact that neither of us looked at all like the two men in the picture didn't seem to bother Billy. He didn't want us to do anything to each other or to him, just to strike and then to hold the exact pose of the men in the magazine. Each month the photograph changes and each month Max and I recreate a different tableau. Billy's taste in scenes isn't particularly kinky—often we don't even have to get hard. Tonight, for example, I lay face-down, spread-eagled on the bed, while Max stood above me unbuttoning his jeans. We never move beyond the static image. Billy only occasionally touches us, he rarely speaks once we're in position, and he doesn't take photographs. Mainly he stands across the room from us and constantly looks back and forth between our tableau and the photograph he holds in his left hand. Presumably he gets off comparing the original and its copy, actually a copy of a copy, but even that's uncertain, since Billy never removes his heavy, obscuring terrycloth robe. Aside from his sexual habits—or perhaps only one of them—all I know of Billy is that he's overweight, middle-aged, balding, and that he lives in a crummy ground-floor apartment in Noe Valley. If the apartment is any indication of his financial situation, the money Billy pays us must take a considerable chunk out of his monthly paycheck.

After Max and I left Billy's apartment that first night, we just stood in the rain looking at one another. "Well," Max finally said, giving the word a Jack Benny drawl. He put his arm around my shoulders, drew me under his umbrella, and we hurried off to his apartment to fuck. We'd been turned on by each other's naked bodies during the session. Max and I were inseparable for two weeks, our affair continued for another month, and then we became best friends. We talk every day, often over dinner, sharing confidences, sharing stories and clients.

We won't share the latter much longer. Max finishes school this semester. In July he'll take his law boards and in the fall he'll join the waspish downtown firm where he worked last summer. And quit hustling.

"WHAT YOU HAVE to understand," I say to Karina as I press the bell, "is that Phillip has this bizarre compulsion to introduce all of his boyfriends to his mother."

We arrange ourselves on large, linen-covered chairs around a circle of glass that's supported by dead cactus trunks. A huge leaded window overlooking the bay reflects the votive candles on the table, and since the night is clear a wash of flickering lights from Oakland and the Berkeley Hills mingles with the candles' flames.

Phillip seats Karina to his right, Barbara Brockman to his left. Barbara is the executive vice president of Phillip's company, and as usual she's dressed and made up to resemble a forties film star, complete with overrouged lips and heavily beaded eyelashes. I am placed between Anne Marie and the architect George Deutsch. The other guests are Barbara's date for the evening Eric Denhault, who's a hunky anesthesiologist with a crooked nose he may have broken playing football or perhaps soccer, since he's French, and Mark, Phillip's current blond of the month.

"Isn't this just lovely," Anne Marie says, waving her hand across the table. Murmurs of admiration for the setting of Baccarat crystal, gold-plated, ivory-handled flatware, blue 1930s California pottery, orange tulips, hand-painted napkins that look like miniatures of the Frankenthaler painting in the living room. Eric Denhault, however, misses Anne Marie's point and says, yes, the views from these old houses on Telegraph Hill are always extraordinary.

"Tam is so clever at these things," Anne Marie says and again waves her hand across the table, certainly attempting to make a new point and perhaps also trying to correct Eric Denhault's misinterpretation of her first one. More murmurs of admiration, including Eric's, as the object of them, Phillip's houseboy, nods modestly and continues serving marinated cod with goat cheese. Anne Marie likes to give the impression that Tam is solely responsible for the perfection of Phillip's decor, his table appointments, his food. In reality every detail, from the exact geometric placement of the Filipino burial urns on the mantel to the slightly below room temperature of the goat cheese, is strictly ordered by Phillip. Tam does the cooking, it's true, but literally under the watchful eyes of Phillip. Phillip never lets Tam set the table when guests are coming; nor would he let me when I lived with him. Anne Marie would have you believe otherwise, apparently feeling that such attention to details is less than masculine and therefore reflects badly on her son. Odd that Phillip's love of housekeeping should bother his mother, while his love of men does not, except perhaps for his *taste* in them. "Oh," was her underwhelmed response when Mark told her over drinks that he was an airline steward. "Well, fly the friendly skies," she said smiling, then turned her back on him. And last year when she was urging me to go to New York to "make my mark" as an actor, Anne Marie confided that she'd always hoped Phillip would find "someone on his own level of achievement."

That "someone" would be hard to come by. When he was in his twenties Phillip founded a computer company that earned him a reputation as an electronic wizard and a very considerable fortune. Unlike a lot of Silicon Valley millionaires, however, Phillip really is smart. He's also handsome but not too handsome, athletic, expensively educated, loyal, generous, decent. In short, excepting his tastes for boys and piss elegance, Phillip is a walking embodiment of all the manly virtues, at least the more conventional ones, a son any mother could be proud of. The very conventionality of Phillip's virtues and their luminous visibility were what made me love him, up to a point, but it was also because of that conventionality, I suppose, that I couldn't love him beyond that point. Also, Phillip is a physical and emotional masochist, the latter of which especially can be trying after a while.

Not that Phillip's masochism is readily visible; not tonight, for example, as he smoothly steers the dinner conversation. I've seen him do this many times before, but I doubt that most of his guests notice how skillfully Phillip takes up conversational slack, how unobtrusively he switches from topic to topic to encompass their various interests, how he asks questions that allow each of them to shine in turn, now getting Karina to talk about her work with Andrei Serban, now getting Eric Denhault to name the best Indian restaurants in London, now getting his mother to tell a funny story about one of her Saint Louis public relations firm's more yahooish clients. It helps, of course, that Phillip has assembled an articulate, tending-toward-loquacious group; only Mark remains relatively silent, and even he gets his moment when the subject turns to opera. He describes a recent awful production of *Salome* and gives a wicked impersonation of the soprano taking her curtain calls amidst boos and hisses.

We argue about the new movies, about Carter's latest feud with Begin, about circumcision ("Well, I'm sorry," Anne Marie says when Phillip weighs in against it, "if only I'd known . . ."; and I catch Karina eyeing Eric Denhault speculatively). We discuss Jean Rhys and Steve Martin, Robert Venturi and Governor Brown, Proposition 13 and Las Vegas. Everyone loves Tam's braciole, the Zen Buddhist restaurant at Fort Mason, and Ingrid Bergman in *Autumn Sonata,* and everyone except George Deutsch loathes Liv Ullman in *Autumn Sonata*. The smooth flow of conversation, the friendly bantering, the smiles and nods of recognition are interrupted often enough to prevent boredom by vehement disagreements, downright rudeness ("Is it really true," Barbara asks Karina, "that you still have to lie down on the casting couch to get a job in television?") and, toward the end of the evening, by drunken sentiments. These range from the lugubrious ("I'm so sorry I won't be here to see you on stage, dear," Anne Marie tells me, taking my hand, and as she says it, means it) to the obscene ("Doesn't Phillip's mother have great tits for a woman her age," Mark announces giddily, fortunately while Anne Marie is in the powder room; Eric Denhault, himself feeling no pain, grins and opens his mouth to respond but is frozen by a look from Barbara that says, "Don't you dare").

The round table encourages general conversation, but from time to time we break into groups of two, three, four. Karina listens intently as Anne Marie, who turns out to be a fan of *Wayne County,* gives thumbnail sketches of that series' characters, the rapes, marriages, divorces, breakdowns they've endured for the last two years. Anne Marie in turn is thrilled to learn about the new character Karina will play and to get a preview of future plot complications. George Deutsch and I continue discussing architecture long after the others' interest in the subject wanes. George has a certain notoriety as a "postmodern" architect ("neoclassical" he corrects me). Actually most of George's buildings that have been constructed—and these he designed in tandem with half a dozen or so others—are standard steel-and-glass highrises. It's difficult, he laments, to get either the big-time firm where he works or individual clients interested in his more progressive designs. Having seen photographs of a prize-winning house George built and drawings and plans for several of his unbuilt ones in the architectural journals, I can understand why. They're garish mixtures of crayon colors, promiscuous blendings of Greek columns, Roman arches, mansard roofs, Bauhaus railings: No, I can't muster much enthusiasm for George's brave new classicism. Nevertheless I like him. I particularly like his curly, unruly black hair, his brown eyes, his deep voice. I say, well, you're still young, isn't architecture supposed to be an old man's profession anyway, and by the time the Coeur à la Crème and the coffee arrive, George's right thigh is pressed against my left one and we're playing footsie under the table.

When Anne Marie excuses herself at ten-thirty to go to bed, the rest of us move back into the living room. Tam follows with a tray of bottles and glasses, and Phillip sets a small mirror and a vial of cocaine on a table in front of the fire. Everyone takes a brandy or cognac, and everyone except Mark does a couple of lines of coke. When Karina says she'd like to see the rest of the house, Phillip happily agrees to show her around. Eric Denhault wants to come with them, George goes to use the bathroom, Mark stretches out on the sofa and closes his eyes. Barbara stares silently into the fire, and, on the stereo, Keith Jarrett picks out a series of discordant notes. It hits. Filtered through drug and drink, the familiar sensation is almost comforting. Ah, yes, the enormous despair! Is it perhaps liberating to see the horror so sharply, to experience that frozen moment, as William Burroughs describes it, when you see what's on the end of every fork?

"Your friend is very beautiful," Barbara finally says.

"Yes, she is."

"She's probably upstairs sucking Eric's cock."

"They're looking at the house. Phillip's with them."

"I don't trust Phillip." Barbara's eyes are very sad.

"Neither should you." I glance at Mark on the sofa.

"Don't worry about that one. He always conks out when he's had too much to drink. But don't trust Phillip."

"Why not?"

"Just don't trust him." She points a red-lacquered fingernail at me. "For your very little own good."

"You're drunk."

"So? I *know*. You didn't get your full amount of money from him last month, did you? Well, did you?"

"Fuck off, Barbara."

I go into the garden room, closing the French doors behind me. The room is dark except for the light of the moon shining through undraped windows, and it's cold. I exhale forcefully but cannot see my breath. I run my palm slowly along my cheek. Is the icy sensation from my hand or from my face—which is colder? I hear the French doors open, then close, then footsteps moving toward me. I feel an arm around my shoulders and turn to George Deutsch. We embrace and kiss, grab each other's crotches, agree to spend the night together.

Karina announces that she wants to go dancing. Eric Denhault enthusiastically seconds her: They also seem to have come to some sort of understanding, stated or unstated, have been casting glances in each other's directions since returning from their tour.

"The Tonga Room!" Phillip cries. Even a secret, in any case seldom-indulged, taste for low camp can't fully explain Phillip's passion for the Tonga Room, a "Polynesian" nightclub in the basement of the Fairmont. The room features a fake lagoon, a moving barge that bears a dance band playing "standards," and—the pièce de résistance—a "rainstorm" once an hour. The clientele are mainly polyestered tourists, suburban teenagers in prom dresses and rented tuxedos, and Phillip's unsuspecting friends. I suggest that if everyone wants to go dancing, we should consider some other alternatives, a guy I know's having a party at The Palms and the Dead Kennedys are playing at Mabuhay Gardens. Besides, men can't dance together at the Fairmont.

"Why not?" Phillip asks. "We'll liberate the Tonga Room. Karina has to see it, you can't come to San Francisco and not."

"Why don't the rest of you just vote on it," Barbara says drily from her ottoman. "I'm tired and want to go home." She—sweetly—smiles up at Eric, who—disingenuously—says that he really wishes she'd come dancing with us, but can understand if she's too tired. Barbara replies—superfluously—that he can, of course, go dancing if he wants. Eric tells her—solicitously—that he'll take her home first and then join the rest of us. Barbara reminds him—sharply—that they came in *her* car.

Karina is trying to suppress a grin. Phillip is trying to wake Mark to get his vote for the Tonga Room. Mark opens unfocused eyes, pushes Phillip away, says, no, no more cognac, vote on what?, no he doesn't want to dance, he just wants to go back to sleep. Phillip, unquestionably more chivalrous than Eric Denhault, decides he'd better skip the dancing too and stay home and get Mark to bed. That leaves four of us, and, after a very brief discussion, we agree that, on balance, we'd rather hear the Dead Kennedys than the dance band at the Tonga Room. I suggest that Karina and Eric can take my car and I'll ride with George.

"How cute," Barbara says, "musical cars." She turns her mouth away when Eric bends to kiss her goodnight.

Phillip stops me at the front door. The others are already on the sidewalk heading toward the street.

"Are you and George . . . ?" Phillip's voice is even, but the twitch of his Adam's apple betrays anxiety or is it irritation?

"But Phillip, I thought the reason you invited George tonight was to meet me. I thought that was the idea."

"Don't be a smartass. I thought he might be able to give you a job."

"I don't want a job."

"Well, we don't always get what we want, do we?"

"No, Phillip, I suppose we don't." I kiss him, at least he doesn't turn his lips away. "Well, thanks again, and give my best to Anne Marie." From the street we hear a squeal as Barbara's Porsche burns rubber.

HEADING NORTH. KARINA says I'm taking the mountain curves too quickly. I say I know the road, not to worry. Karina grunts. We're going to look at the redwoods in Muir Woods, the last of our tourist outings. Karina leaves tomorrow.

As I drive, I run lines, Karina cues me. She says she likes what I'm doing, but wonders if I've done enough emotional work? Despite Karina's ballet and mime classes, her training in diction and the English classical style, her experiments with Brechtian and Grotowskian and oriental theater, in the end she is, like most American actors, a religious adherent of "the Method" and its attendant "emotional work." As am I. I assure her that I've done my emotional work, but Karina's not convinced I've done enough, thinks that Jean could use more shades of feeling than I'm giving him. Do I detect her patronizing me, the professional speaking to the amateur? And why not? I am an amateur, she a professional. I say, well maybe she's right, maybe I should do some more emotional work, and Karina says she thinks that would be helpful.

Shades of feeling in the very air around us, shifting moods as the sun plays hide and seek. When it disappears behind the banks of fog hanging over the ocean, the light turns pearly gray, and we're suspended high above the world in a private space, time out of mind. As the sun breaks through the clouds, the water glimmers, the cliffs are washed in golden warmth, and the world, the real world stretches below us, around us, ours to seize. We're both immensely pleased. Impossible to capture the duality of nature's show, Karina says, but she wants to have at least some record. Twice I pull the car off the road for her to photograph the swirling mass of ocean to our left and the rolling hills covered with heather to our right. At one stop I cross a low, barbed-wire fence, scramble up an embankment, and pull bunches of heather from the ground by their roots. I lift the purple blossoms and their greenery high above my head as a boxer lifts his trophy.

By the time we arrive at Muir Woods the sun has disappeared completely, the rains have come. Steam rises from the damp ground, enhancing the sense of being in a primordial forest, and the ancient redwoods, gnarled and stretching skyward, are both sheltering and somehow threatening. Our excitement about the setting is, however, tempered by the cold, the rain, which falls steadily if lightly, and the crowd. Other tourists clog the narrow paths through the groves. You repeatedly hear a metallic click and a rustle of fabric as your umbrella collides with someone else's. Well better that, you think, than being crowded against a sweaty stranger.

I remember walking through a crowd on a hot summer day in Turner Falls. I must have been about ten or eleven, and I must have been on some sort of family excursion. The only relative I recall clearly from that day, though, is my Aunt Em. As we passed an enormous wall of water cascading from a rocky ledge, I pointed and asked loudly, "Who made all this?" I knew what Aunt Em's answer would be. She was the only one in the family who attended church regularly, the rest of us went only on Easter and sometimes to the candlelight service on Christmas Eve, and my question, although posed solemnly enough, was really meant sarcastically. I hated church as much as I did school, and I knew, without ever giving it much thought, that there was no such thing as God. I suppose I wanted to reconfirm my own worst suspicions about Aunt Em's character or perhaps to expose her contemptible piety to the listening crowd. "The Good Lord, of course," my Aunt Em answered, "the Good Lord," but she spoke with such gravity and with such enormous sadness that I was pierced. The hairs rise on the back of my neck when I think of Aunt Em's voice that day, my face still burns with shame.

After half an hour we decide we've seen enough redwoods and head back to the canteen for coffee and hot dogs.

Karina: "I'm almost thirty, although thank God I don't look it, but I *am* three years older than you, maybe that's the difference. I know thirty's not really old, but for an actress it certainly ain't young. About a year ago I started getting really worried about the future—I mean I'd always been worried about the future, the bomb and all that—but personally worried. Often in the morning I'd wake up scared, really terrified, has that ever happened to you? I'd been working in 'serious' theater for eight years, and here I was still waitressing and demonstrating products and collecting unemployment and living in that horrid little apartment. Speaking of which, did I tell you about the woman in my building who was murdered by her boyfriend? I read about it in the newspaper. I was passing a newsstand, and there it was, this huge photograph of my building on the front page of the *Daily News,* with a black arrow pointing to her window on the fourth floor. I never knew them. Anyway, I saw the life I was leading stretching on forever, and I couldn't see that, I just couldn't deal with it. I realized I was tired, Cal, so tired of being 'dedicated,' and I decided to make some money. So I got a couple of commercials and finally this crappy TV series.

"Did you know I had to sign a contract for three years? Of course, if I'm a success on the show my agent says I can renegotiate the contract for more money, for a *lot* more money, and I guess that's what I want, but I can't get out of it. After that maybe I can go on to movies, the name recognition and all that's supposed to help. That's the other thing I've realized, what I've always really wanted was to be a movie star. Actress hell, I want to be a star. Not that it's so easy moving from TV to movies. Of course, there are Goldie Hawn and Farrah Fawcett, but all of Farrah's movies have been flops, not that she doesn't make a killing pushing perfume and shampoo.

"Can you believe it's come to this? Here I am talking about Farrah Fawcett and you're telling me you hide all your books in that little room so your . . ."

"Customers."

"So your customers will think you're stupid. Who knew?"

In the darkness we're driving south, heading home.

"Did you ever see *California Split,* Karina?"

"No."

"George Segal and Elliott Gould are these down-on-their-luck gamblers, but at the end of the movie they finally win a fortune in Reno. At which point Gould turns to Segal and says, 'It's over. I'm going home,' and Segal asks, 'Oh yeah, where do you live?' "

AN INTERVIEW WITH a therapist. Dr. Redman has, appropriately enough, curly red hair and a florid complexion. Equally appropriately, he today wears a red and white tattersall shirt and a red raw-silk tie. His bright blue eyes study me closely from behind tortoiseshell-framed glasses.

Q: You say it's not your work that's bothering you?

A: No.

Q: You never mind having to sell your body?

A: There are hassles, as in all jobs, that's normal, isn't it? But nothing more than that. By the way, I don't *have* to sell my body, as you put it, I do it because I want to.

Q: Why?

A: Why what?

Q: Why did you become a prostitute?

A: It's an easy way to make money.

54

Q: You make a lot?

A: Enough.

Q: Your rates are certainly high enough.

A: As are yours.

Q: Touché. You wouldn't, though, rather be doing something more, uh, socially useful, if you'll forgive the term?

A: No.

Q: Nothing?

A: I'm working on it, okay? What's socially useful anyway?

Q: Why so defensive? We'll go into that.

A: Look, I could give you some hackneyed argument about the needs the oldest profession fulfills and all that, but I assume you're too intelligent for that. But I'm serious. Should I rather be pushing a lot of useless papers? Or pretending to help poor people while feathering my own bureaucratic nest? Or building nuclear weapons?

Q: You stack the cards by using extreme examples. You're political then?

A: No. Talk about socially useless.

Q: Are you a punk?

A: What?

Q: An interesting attitude, this new nihilism. So many young people seem to share it, and older people too, I suppose, if they knew it. I'm not necessarily saying you're wrong.

A: I'm sure as hell not a philosopher.

Q: But you quoted Nietzsche earlier.

A: Actually I didn't quote him. I paraphrased. Like everyone else, I went to college.

Q: Tell me about your parents.

A: I'm an orphan.

Q: Extremely interesting.

A: (Silence)

Q: Well, we'll go into that. Do you have a lover?

A: No.

Q: No one you see regularly?

A: A few people. Some of them clients.

Q: And some not?

A: That's right.

Q: You have a lot of casual sex?

A: Depends on what you mean by casual. If you mean bars and baths and stuff, no.

Q: Why is that?

A: After you've done two or three tricks a day, you're not exactly in the mood to run off to the baths.

Q: No, I suppose you wouldn't be. Doesn't it bother you, in hustling, never being in control of the situation?

A: But I am in control of the situation. Always. That's what I like about it.

Q: Yes, I can see that. But what I meant was, doesn't it bother you not being able to choose whom you have sex with?

A: I do choose. I mean, I don't just accept everyone who calls. But I see what you mean, in that sense I'm passive. No, it doesn't bother me.

Q: You never see someone on the street that

you'd rather be having sex with than one of the people who calls you on the phone?

A: Sure. Sometimes I do have sex with people I meet on the street, usually not. But that's normal. Don't you see people on the street you want to fuck and can't? Everyone cruises constantly. It's not just gay. Did you ever read Baudelaire? He talks about constantly falling in love with these women he sees on his walks around the city. Falling in love for a minute or two.

Q: You said "passive" just now. But I assume you're sexually "active."

A: I both fuck and get fucked, if that's what you mean.

Q: When I was young, you know, you couldn't do both. You had to choose. Either active or passive. Butch or femme.

A: (Silence)

Q: Well, it's much better now, I think. And, of course, that's perfect for me. I need someone versatile. To get into that, what sort of problems do your clients have?

A: Problems?

Q: Sexual problems?

A: Christ, you don't expect me to recommend people to you, do you?

Q: No, of course not. I'm just interested in knowing if you've ever dealt with any of the same kinds of problems that might come up with my patients.

A: Like what?

Q: Impotence, for example.

A: I've run into that, but it's not something I focus on. On the contrary.

Q: With my patients, of course, that's the idea. We focus on the problem. What about fetishes?

A: Yes?

Q: They don't bother you?

A: I don't do scat, I don't get fisted, and I don't get beaten. Anything else goes.

Q: Bondage? Torture? Toys? Piss? Games? Fantasies?

A: Anything goes.

Q: Splendid.

Dr. Redman approached me about being a sex surrogate, but when I found out how much he paid, less than half my hourly rate, I told him to forget it. He insisted that I take down his number, just in case, and a week later I called him back. My proposition to him, which he's now accepted, is that I work as a sex surrogate for one hour a week in exchange for which he'll see me for one hour a week of (nonsexual) therapy. Since his hourly rate is twenty-five dollars more than mine, I come out ahead. I've managed to convince him that I'm worth more than he pays his other surrogates, that I'll be especially useful with his more difficult cases. I've managed to convince myself that Dr. Redman will help me understand why I wake up every morning scared.

•-•-•-•-**13**•-•-•-•-•

WHEN I PHONE Phillip to invite him to the opening of
Miss Julie, Diana, his secretary, tells me that he's out
of town. For how long? Three weeks. Where? The Far
East. *The Far East?* Mainly in Hong Kong, but he'll be
going on to Tokyo. When will he be back? Not for
another two and a half weeks, he just left on Wednesday.

Odd that Phillip didn't tell me about this trip. I
haven't seen him since his dinner for Anne Marie
three weeks ago, but in the past he would have let me
know if he was going to be away for so long. Key
phrase that: in the past. I haven't called Phillip just to
invite him to the play, I want to find out why my
check for this month hasn't arrived yet. Is that also in
the past?

I ask Diana to transfer me to Barbara Brockman,
who'll tell me why Phillip's in Hong Kong and I hope
offer some clue as to what's going on with him,
regarding me. Not that I intend to mention the check
to Barbara. Her secretary puts me on hold, then

comes back on the line to say that Barbara's "in conference." No, she doesn't know when Barbara will be free. Do I wish to leave my number? No. May she tell Barbara what this is in reference to? No.

Maybe Phillip mailed the check before he left, and I'll receive it tomorrow. Don't fool yourself, baby. You're going to have to take money out of your savings account to pay the rent. Is this the end of my benefactor then? Already upset by my meeting with Jimmy this morning, and now further depressed by Phillip's unreliability, I put on the stereo headset and place the needle toward the middle of Billy Joel's *52nd Street* album. I want to hear him sing "My Life," but I miscalculate the bands and get the end of "Honesty," a sappy love song. When Billy Joel finally comes on strong about the man who gives a stand-up routine in LA, I turn up the volume and sing along.

Let the phone ring. It continues doing so. I consider unplugging it, but I just lost a thousand bucks, so to speak, so after ten rings I pick up the receiver. Max is on the line, wants to know why I'm not answering my phone? But I *am* answering, Max. What am I doing anyway, is a trick there? No, I'm lying on my bed, alone, listening to Billy Joel. You've got terrible taste in music, Cal. Yeah, you've said that before, I mean, I've heard it *enough.* Touchy, Cal, touchy.

Max wants to know if I can do a double with him tonight at the Huntington, some guy in from Dallas. I say he'd better not count on me, Kline has been keeping us later and later at rehearsals. Max asks what else is happening. I tell him about Phillip being in Hong Kong, about the missing check, about Barbara Brockman giving me the cold shoulder. I hang up without, however, mentioning my meeting this morning with Jimmy. In fact, although Max and I always tell each other about our tricks, both the paying and the nonpaying ones, I haven't yet said anything to him at all about Jimmy Black.

Of course, Jimmy's not a "trick" exactly. Nor do "client" or "patient" seem quite the right words to describe a sweet-natured, good-looking, twenty-one-year-old San Francisco State business major whose "sexual dysfunction" I am, under Dr. Redman's guidance, attempting to help overcome. Following a get-acquainted session two weeks ago and a touching-with-clothes-on session last week, today Jimmy and I met to give each other nonsexual—or at least nongenital—massages. Throughout those first two meetings in a room next to Dr. Redman's office, I had the distinct and distinctly uneasy sensation that the doctor was watching Jimmy and me, perhaps through some sort of hidden peephole. This morning, thank God, I didn't have to worry about that. For, following the instructions Dr. Redman always gives me beforehand, the first thing I did after greeting Jimmy was to turn off the overhead lights of the small windowless room. The darkness, Dr. Redman had explained, was intended to eliminate all visual stimulation. He had also said that Jimmy and I should avoid *verbal* stimulation today. That is, we shouldn't talk. Well, when I first turned out the lights, we didn't talk, but we did giggle nervously, like two little boys alone in the dark, self-consciously aware of their own naughtiness.

When I finally reached out for Jimmy my right hand touched material, stiff cotton. I moved my fingers down what I recognized as the sleeve of a starched shirt until I found the bare flesh of Jimmy's wrist and took his hand in mine. I pulled his other hand to me, and for several minutes we stood motionless except for the play of palms pressing against palms, fingers intertwining.

Then I drew Jimmy closer to me, rubbed the back of his neck, ruffled his thick hair. I ran my hand across his forehead, his bushy eyebrows, closed eyelids, large nose, the rough stubble of a day-old growth of beard, and Jimmy tentatively kneaded the back of my neck. Coarse chest hairs tickled the sides of my fingers as I undid six buttons. I helped Jimmy out of his shirt, and he helped me pull my T-shirt over my head.

I turned Jimmy away from me, pressed my hands against the back of his neck, already moist with sweat, against his shoulders, against the muscles of his back. His skin smelled of fear and Dial soap. I massaged his ass through his jeans and the backs of his thighs and calves. When I stood up and turned him to face me again, Jimmy was breathing noisily, I could feel his hot breath against my face.

"Are you okay?" I whispered, temporarily ignoring Dr. Redman's prohibitions.

"I'm okay."

"You better take off your jeans yourself." I heard him unzip and slip out of his pants and shoes as I slipped out of mine. When I stepped back toward Jimmy, I grazed his coarse chest hair with my left elbow, accidentally bumped my thigh against his. Jimmy quickly pulled away, but, grabbing his arm and moving my leg back against his, I signaled him to hold our side-by-side stance. Muscled thigh worked against muscled thigh, now increasing, now decreasing the pressure. Then suddenly Jimmy jerked away again, screamed.

"You didn't . . ."

"Yes, goddammit," he said, angry, disgusted. Once again, he'd come prematurely. I placed my arms around Jimmy's slumped shoulders. I held him in the dark.

I TELL JULIE that I won't continue living in her father's house. Beneath my words lie weeks of delving into my own bitter leavetakings. Such as the day Michael Worth kicked me out of his house and the next day when I returned to slash his furniture with a kitchen knife. Such as watching *Ship of Fools* on television and listening to Susan weep in the next room the night she found out I didn't love her. Such as Tam's noncommittal "Good-bye" as he put my suitcases in the taxi waiting at Phillip's front door. Such as the single word Odus spoke, "Good," when I told him I wasn't coming back to Oklahoma, ever again.

I tell Julie that I can no longer bow and scrape. I know the humiliation of being a servant because I know the humiliations of being a hustler, a kept boy, a maker of boxes, and an actor who is, more often than not, a pawn in the hands of an egomaniac.

I tell Julie that I'll make her a countess, I explain my plan to open a luxurious hotel in Switzerland. Here I've drawn on my childhood dreams and on only partially answered adult prayers. Growing up in an ugly farmhouse, I fantasized that I lived in mansions whose pictures I'd clipped from magazines. I saw myself moving from one gorgeous house to another, wearing expensive clothes, trailing clouds of money, meeting the rich and famous. I thought of making love to Marlon Brando and Elizabeth Taylor. Ten years later, at a party with Michael Worth, I actually did meet Elizabeth Taylor, although I didn't make love to her. And later I did live in houses like those I'd dreamed about, although these were not, as I'd planned, my own: rather, Michael's, Phillip's.

Every word I speak, every step I take, every movement of my arm, my neck, my eyes, each represents a distillation of diverse sights, sounds, smells. The puzzled look on my childhood sweetheart's face as I pushed her down on a bed and pressed my bulging pants against her thigh. The clump of Daddy's boots coming toward me as I cowered under a card table. The aphrodisiacal scent of a perfume Susan wore called My Sin. The orange melancholy of a deserted country road at sunset. These memories that I've dug up weeks before—archaeologists of the emotions we! —float at the back of my consciousness, completely at my disposal. No need to focus on them individually at this point. They work collectively now, enhancing, rather than intruding upon, my present objectives: to get Julie to notice me, to seduce her, to make her cry, to convince her to kill herself.

My carefully-plotted objectives are themselves subsumed in the emotional current flowing between Julie and me and, on a different plane, between us and the audience. I don't look out into the auditorium, of course, but I know they're with us. There's none of that struggling against a bad crowd when you feel as though you're moving under water. There's no coughing, no rustling, no dead silence. No: Tonight the silence is alive, attentive, pregnant.

"Oh my God," Julie cries, "what have I done? My God!"

"So that's what you're singing *now?* What have you done? What many others have done before you."

Julie screams hysterically. "And now you despise me! I'm falling—falling—"

"Fall low enough—fall down to my level—then I'll raise you up again." No need for me to summon up either brutality or the faint hint of compassion. They simply come, like breathing. I'm alive here, I can actually feel myself living tonight.

GEORGE DEUTSCH AND I are sitting on a bed in Linda's apartment in the Mission, drinking cheap red wine and eating nachos with guacamole dip. Four strangers sit on the floor nearby, but a stereo speaker between them and us, now blasting out Nina Hagen, creates, in effect, a wall of sound, allowing us to ignore them, they us. Occasionally someone from the crew wanders into the room, yells congratulations at me, then heads to the rear of the apartment where the action is. From that direction a cacophony of voices competes with and sometimes drowns out Nina Hagen's shouts. George offers to come with me if I want to go back and be sociable, but I'm not one for theatrical camaraderie, especially not tonight. George says, for the second time, that it's too bad we can't dance. I agree, but one of Linda's roommates has already announced that dancing is off limits, the floor might collapse. Apparently at the last party they gave, the downstairs neighbor arrived with the cops and with huge chunks of plaster that had fallen from his ceiling.

Kline appears at the bedroom door, gnawing on an already half-eaten chicken leg. Seeing us, he motions with the chicken leg for me to join him. I tell George I'll be right back and follow Kline through a hall and into a tiny Victorian water closet. When Kline closes the door, we're practically in each other's arms.

"Goddamn noise out there," Kline grunts. I look into his unsmiling face. The light from a bare overhead bulb causes him to squint even more than usual. Very slowly he begins nodding his head up and down.

"Good job. Your heart was in it."

"And my guts."

"You deserve the award for the most improved actor." What can you do with a backhanded compliment like that, other than accept it?

"Thanks." Kline takes another bite of chicken, chews noisily.

"I want you to try out for my next play. In August. It's an original by Mickey Martin, he calls it *The Green Stranger*. You just might work."

"Okay. Thanks." Kline throws the now-bare bone out an open window into an airshaft and without another word he leaves the tiny room.

After a polite stay of an hour, George and I head to the I-Beam to dance. There I hand the doorman a twenty for the cover charges, and only after we've made our way across the crowded lounge and I reach for my wallet at the bar, do I realize that the doorman didn't give me the fifteen dollars I was due in change. While George takes care of the drinks, I return to get my money. The doorman, however, a pretty-boy type of twenty, feigns ignorance. Impossible, he says, that I gave him a twenty, he'd have remembered. Impossible

my ass, I tell him, and I'm sure he *does* remember.
There wasn't a line when we arrived, which means
that no more than a couple of people, if any, could
have gone past him since us, so it's not like there's
some *confusion* about where the twenty came from.
So I want my fifteen bucks back. Where is it, in his
pocket? Don't insult me, he says. That, I say, would be
impossible. At which point the bouncer, a three-
hundred-pound ape, appears from the shadows. Unfortunately I've had dealings with him before. When
he scowls at me and asks pretty boy what's the matter,
I know I'll never see that fifteen dollars. I turn my
back on them and walk. In the middle of the lounge, I
turn briefly, yell, "What do you two motherfuckers do
anyway, split the graft?" then continue across the
room. "That's it for you, punk," the bouncer thunders
at my back, and I fully expect to feel his big paws on
my shoulders before I reach the bar. But I don't.
Maybe the ape remembers that I know his boss.

"Did you get your money?" George asks.

"No, I almost got a fat lip though."

"Figures. Let's go to the bathroom and do another
line."

George and I have gone out together and gone to
bed together a couple of times since we met at
Phillip's. Certainly no need for possessiveness there.
The kid George is dancing with has very short legs, a
handsome Italian profile, and curly black hair to go
with the profile. His tightly-muscled torso, streaked
with sweat, gleams beneath the amber spotlights. The
kid dances with wild abandon, and he's very, very
good. George's dancing, by contrast, is a bit tame for
the Ramones.

I take the beer the man has ordered for me and down half of it in one gulp. I like the man's face, large but thin, with a prominent nose, slanting, almost Asiatic eyes, deep lines cut into the tan around the mouth and across the forehead. I like the way he's dressed. His crisp white shirt, burgundy tie, and gray Armani suit stand out among bodies that are either shirtless or T-shirted. And I like the man's deep voice and his big body. I'm not sure I like his name though. Sport Milliken. He says he's in town for the weekend from Los Angeles, and he wants me to come back with him to his room at the Fairmont. I like his direct approach. I explain that I'm with a friend. Yes, he's been watching us dance. He wants us both to come to his room, he's willing to pay us each $250. I open my mouth to protest, but before I can think of what to say, Sport grins, says, well you are a hustler, aren't you? If not, you should be, all men as handsome as you should be when they're young. I grin. Even if I am, I say, my friend certainly isn't. Check him out, Sport urges, you might be surprised.

I am surprised. George is excited by the promise of an orgy, flattered by Sport's proposition. But he wants to bring along his new friend Mark. The kid told George that he wanted to be fucked by him, and who, George asks, could resist that fine Italian ass? Okay by me, I say, as long as we don't tell the kid about the money. Sport nods. We'll see what Mark has to say.

For three hours we've been flowing into various combinations of two, three, four, fueled by a Quaalude each and by periodic helpings of coke and poppers. And by champagne. When the middle-aged waiter brought in the first magnum he didn't bat an eye at the sight of four naked men in various stages of erection. The waiter who brought in the second magnum was equally nonchalant. I wonder if the first waiter warned him? And I picture a whole relay of waiters bringing champagne, each standing in the bowels of the hotel as his predecessors grin mysteriously and say, take this to 1251, check it out. Of course, it's possible that four naked men in various stages of erection is a not uncommon sight at the Fairmont.

Feeling the first stages of exhaustion, I rest on the chaise and watch the others on the bed. George and Sport are attempting to fuck the kid at the same time. We've all taken to calling Mark "the kid." Unfortunately—unfortunately for this particular operation—George and Sport both have big cocks and can't keep them together inside the kid's ass for more than a few seconds at a time. Finally conceding defeat, the three roll apart and collapse in a fit of giggles. "Now let's get serious," Sport says and laughs some more. But he remounts Mark. George comes to me, sticks out his tongue and, leaving it in the air, bends and thrusts it in my mouth. Pressing me against his hairy chest, he lifts and carries me to the bed. There he drops me. He slides his cock into Sport's ass while Sport continues to thrust into Mark. Turning his head toward me, sticking poppers under my nose, George indicates that he wants me to do the same for him. I signal for him to wait, my cock's not hard. As I work on it with my hand, the Valkyries enter again. All night the tape machine on the nightstand has been playing Wagner. How appropriate. Perfect really.

* * *

"Do you think he was serious about taking us with him to Mustique?"

"One night as a hustler, George, and already you're all set to be flown to the Caribbean."

"I don't know. You don't think he really has a place there?" Under the streetlamp George studies the card Sport handed him as we left. Sport handed me one too, and he told us to call him the next time we're in LA.

"Sport Milliken Productions. Do you suppose he does films? Maybe he'll get you a job in a movie."

"And maybe he'll hire you to build him a house."

"All right, all right. I had a terrific time though, didn't you?" The Gothic spires of Grace Cathedral cast moonlit shadows to our left, and the night air is cool and clean and velvety after the rain. Yeah, I had a terrific time.

·—·—·— 16 ·—·—·—

IT HITS ON the running track on my fourteenth lap. Dr. Redman, who's even more of a fool than I originally thought, has suggested that I make lists, lists of "positives" to counterbalance what he refers to as my "depression." Oddly this foolish trick often works. If it works, does that then mean that it's not foolish?

Okay. *Miss Julie* closed last night, perhaps a negative in itself, certainly the last performance was accompanied by a sense of letdown. But, and here's the positive, Kline stopped me as I left the stage and said again that he wants me to audition for *The Green Stranger*. Generous of Kline considering that in contrast to their glowing appreciations of his and Linda's contributions, the reviewers were uniformly negative about my performance in *Miss Julie*. The wittiest among them described me as belonging to "the Tab Hunter school of beauty carved in wood." If you call that wit.

Positive two. Phillip came to see the play and said

he was "impressed." Two days later I received a check from him in the mail that covers this month's rent as well as July's and August's. Unsolicited. I had decided not to mention the missing check to him, hoping that Phillip would bring it up himself eventually. I didn't expect the resolution to our money problem to come so easily though. Unexpected manna. I phoned Phillip to thank him and agreed to go with him to a Bobby Short concert next Friday.

Three, not unrelated to Phillip's rekindled generosity, I've bought myself a new car. With the money from my savings account I thought I'd have to use to pay my rent for the next few months, I made a down payment on a fresh-from-the-factory Honda Accord LX, a gray coupe with a black racing stripe and black interior. Not the classiest car in the world but a definite improvement over my beat-up MG. It has a sunroof, power steering, power windows, air conditioning, tape deck, stereo speakers.

Four, at the beginning of my session yesterday with Jimmy Black, our eighth, he shyly confessed that the exercises we've been doing together—more and more successfully—gave him the courage to go out to a bar last weekend. He went home with a guy he met at Moby Dick, and the sex they had together was just fine. "I mean," Jimmy said, "I think he wanted me to wait a little longer than I did to come, but still . . ." Jimmy laughed. "If he only knew . . ." and Jimmy smiled at me, a smile of gratitude and, in a sense, of love.

Five? Positive five? Well, Max gave me a cactus, an elaborate spiny affair that's supposed to bloom next winter. I have a history of letting plants die, including two of Max's bromeliads when he was in Hawaii last March. "There's *no way,*" he said, "you can kill this one."

This is getting foolish. I'll round it up, so, positive six, it's an incredibly beautiful day. Large windows border the running track on three sides, north, east, south, offering me a panorama of a cloudless blue sky above pastel, Mediterranean tints. In the distance rise downtown's towers of commerce, their rectangular slabs abruptly punctuated by the needle-thin top of the Transamerica Pyramid. Further north, on Nob Hill, stand older and more graceful masses, with a large American flag atop the Mark Hopkins waving slowly, slowly in the wind. Closer in, just across the corner from the gym, sits a small Mission Revival style church that's famous for its rousing gospel services on Sunday and for its equally rousing social-ist meetings the rest of the week. To the south of the gym there's a beige brick, zigzag modern highrise that was also originally a religious building, put up, oddly enough, by the Methodist Church in the twenties. Even odder, at one point in its history, the building's street-level chapel was balanced by a nightclub on its rooftop penthouse. Symbolically, shouldn't those po-sitions have been reversed?

Positive seven. By my twentieth lap around the track, my anxiety has leveled down to nothing.

Men stroll in the sun on Castro Street, as do a few women, even a child. The little girl's stroller is pushed by a tall bearded man in standard Castro drag— Levi's, a T-shirt—who gives me the eye as I pass. Is the man the child's father, and is this what it seems? Is he really using his daughter as some sort of cruising come-on?

Many of the men here today came to San Francisco —and specifically they came to the Castro—looking for paradise, and perhaps some of them have found it. Others, like me, came here on vacation and ended up staying. Maybe some of them have also found paradise. Perhaps others, like me, stayed because the place allows you to drift so pleasantly, allows the past and old hopes, ambitions to travel further and further out before disappearing, perhaps forever, beyond the horizon. Actually, I came here for the most banal of all reasons, to get over the end of a love affair.

A story: I met Michael Worth when he came to New Haven to play Coriolanus at the Yale Rep. After the play's closing-night party, Michael and I went to bed together, and the next morning he told me to look him up when I came to New York. That was when I still took people seriously when they told me to look them up, and when I moved to New York after graduation that spring, I phoned Michael. Naturally I got his answering service, but within an hour he returned my call. We had dinner that night, and a month later I moved from the floor of a friend's apartment on East Sixth Street to Michael's townhouse off Gramercy Park. And I moved into Michael's world of money, famous names, the theater. I quit looking for a job with an architectural firm and became his "secretary." At his urging, I began taking acting classes, dance classes, voice lessons. Michael's agent even took me on, as a favor to him, of course, and I got a small part in a play at LaMama, which is where I met Karina. Then I got a part in a revival of *The Jew of*

Malta and another part in a play at the American Place Theater and a television commercial (which was never aired) for a new brand of hot cereal.

My affair with Michael ended as banally as it began. He returned home unexpectedly one night to find me in bed with a black man I'd picked up at the Ninth Circle, and he kicked me out right then. Two days later, jobless, homeless, and not a little concerned about how Michael was reacting to having his furniture slashed, I caught a plane to San Francisco, thinking I'd spend the summer here "getting my head together" and return to New York and to my new-found acting career in the fall. But that was three years ago, and, as Marlowe says, that was in another country, and, as Marlowe also says, besides, the wench is dead.

17

Dear Cal,

I'm sorry that I've been out of touch for so long, and I'm covered with embarrassment that I never wrote to thank you properly for the wonderful time you showed me in April. But I presume you got my flowers on opening night? How did that go?

My excuse is that I've been terribly busy—not a real excuse I know. But "Wayne County" 's shooting schedule is rough, up every morning at six, in bed by ten, but then everyone assures me that's true of all series. The people on the show are much better than I expected, and I seem to be doing okay—at least no one's talking about replacing me yet. And—this is my really exciting news—it looks like I'm actually going to be in a movie. A remake of an old gangster film called "The Rise and Fall of Legs Diamond." Did you ever see it? If so, I'm to play the young innocent girl at the beginning who gets led down the crimson path. My agent out *here's been negotiating and it's almost set. I can do it because they'll be filming during the break of "Wayne County" 's shooting schedule. Cross your fingers for me. It's low-budget but still a* movie.

I've found a wonderful apartment. In the "old" part of Hollywood. You'll love it, it even has a Barbara Stanwyck staircase leading from my bedroom down to the living room! Perfect for grand entrances. Which leads me to—I really wish you'd consider coming down to LA, moving here I mean. Now maybe I'm way out of line here, but you seemed sort of directionless when I saw you. I can understand why you don't want to go back to New York—who does?—but you know as well as I do that you've either got to be there or here if you're serious about acting. I know you profess to be serious about nothing, but you are *acting again, so why not give LA a try. I'm sure with your looks—and let's face it a lot out here is based on looks, but so, I assume, is what you're doing now, so why should that bother you? Anyway, with your looks and your stage credits—including the current one—I'm sure you'd be able to find an agent. Contrary to popular opinion, they* do *want people to have some stage experience. People don't seem to be discovered in drugstores anymore, if they ever were. I could recommend you to my agent. Because as you know, I really do think you're a good actor, even if you don't. Other people do too. Remember what Mira Rostova said? I'm sure you're (were?) terrific as Jean. And of course this may all sound absurd, since there you are doing Strindberg and here I am doing pulp. But on the other hand, we've all got to make a living, so why not make it doing something you're doing any-way? And, I can hear you say—cynically—"and make it doing something respectable," but you know I don't give a damn about that. I do worry about you though, I've been thinking about you a lot. Don't take this wrong, but you didn't seem terribly happy when I saw you. ?*

So will you consider coming down here, if only for a visit, or to try it out? You can stay with me, of course, for as long as you need to.

I miss you.

> *Much love,*
> *Karina*

THE HOUSE SITS in an isolated grove of trees, high up in the Berkeley Hills. It could have been designed by Maybeck during his Swiss Chalet period. Maybeck on an off day though, for its shingled roof is too steep and its overhanging eaves are too dramatic for the small structure, and an elaborate bay window is ill-placed, too far to one side of the wooden front. Despite these

flaws of proportion the house is handsome and pos-
sesses an undeniable period charm, a charm enhanced
by the place's slight but definite air of decay. Large
evergreen shrubs, badly in need of pruning, scrape the
sides of my car on the steep, narrow driveway, and
wild grass grows from the cracks in the cobblestone
path that leads from the driveway to the front door.

The man who greets me is tall and overweight and
of indeterminate age. He could be thirty, or forty-five.
He has hair so pale and skin so white that, except for
his small blue eyes, he might be taken for an albino.
He wears double-knit slacks, a blue sports shirt, and
maroon-colored carpet slippers. His voice is small,
affectless.

The front door opens directly into a large room that
must take up the house's entire ground floor. We enter
the double-height half of the room, which is carpeted
in orange shag and is furnished with worn Danish
modern pieces that contrast unpleasantly with the
grandeur of oak ceiling beams, a massive stone fireplace, the bay window. Striped fiberglass curtains
cover the window, and the fireplace, obviously un-
used, is filled with stacks of newspapers and magazines. The only decorations are a couple of pots of ivy
hanging in macramé holders from the ceiling beams
and a needlepoint wall hanging with the legend BLESS
THIS HOUSE. At the room's opposite end, the kitchen
has been "modernized" with white metal cupboards
and speckled Formica. On the counter separating the
two areas sits an unfinished Colonel Sanders' fried
chicken dinner. He wants to know if I mind if he
finishes his supper. I say I don't mind and sit down on
one of the plastic-covered bar stools.

He asks about the drive from the city, and I say the

drive was fine. I tell him how much I like his place and ask when it was built, but he has no knowledge of and apparently no interest in the house's history. He says he's been renting it for a little over a year. That exhausts our conversation, neither of us really wants to talk. So I sit in silence as he eats his fried chicken and mashed potatoes, the latter with a plastic fork that comes with the dinner.

He sweeps the red and white striped bag, the matching cardboard container, and the paper plates into a wastebasket and says he's going to brush his teeth, he'll be right back. The wooden stairs to the left of the kitchen creak beneath his weight. I might as well leave right now, I can sense he's going to try to rip me off. He's not the type who can afford my rates, especially my rates for the whole night, which is what he insisted he wanted when he phoned. Of course, appearances can be deceiving. I'll wait until he comes back down, but I'll ask for the money before we do anything. That's unusual but then so is he.

When he returns, he's changed into a plaid flannel robe.

"So let's get with it," he says, his voice, as before, devoid of emotion.

"Do you think maybe we could settle on the money first?"

"I thought we settled that on the phone."

"Yes, but I mean could you pay me now?"

"Don't you trust me?"

"I just think it would work out better if you gave me the money first." He stares at me. Do I detect the first flicker of emotion behind the pale blue eyes? "Do you have the money?" He doesn't answer, which means he hasn't got it. I knew it. "Look, if you're not willing to

81

pay me now, I'm leaving." I rise from the stool, but he just continues, maddeningly, to stare at me. "You don't have it, do you? Do you? Asshole, I drove all the way over here and you don't even have the fucking money. I ought to beat the shit out of you." We face each other across the counter and, without breaking his gaze and before I realize what's happening, he's reached into a drawer, pulled out a small pistol, and pointed it at me. My fist stops in mid-air.

"Okay, look man, I wasn't really going to hurt you. Just calm down. You don't need that gun." Maybe the gun's not loaded, but maybe it is. His face remains expressionless. I start inching away from him, toward the door, making sure to keep my eyes on the gun.

"Stop." I stop.

"Look man, this isn't going to work. Let's just forget the whole thing, okay? No hard feelings?"

"Move toward the center of the room, over by the fireplace." I hesitate momentarily, then do what he says. "Now get undressed."

"Please." I hear my voice cracking.

"Get undressed." I undress. He moves out from behind the counter, comes forward, all the time keeping the gun aimed at me.

"Play with yourself." I look around the room for some object large enough to crack his skull, but there's nothing in sight, and even if there were, how would I get to it? I take hold of my cock. With his free hand he pulls a small Kodak from the pocket of his robe. Jesus Christ.

"Look, if you're going to take pictures, would you mind just photographing me from the waist down? Please?"

"Sure." For the first time he smiles. His teeth are

small and very white. "Now get with it." I try. When the flash goes off, I'm blinded and experience a split second of terror, unsure whether the flash came from the gun or the camera. I'm still alive. He takes another picture, then tells me to turn around. I can't. It's scary enough facing the gun, I'm not going to turn around and be shot in the back.

"I said turn around."

"Please don't shoot me."

"I'm not going to shoot you if you do what I want. Now move."

"Promise?" Very slowly I turn away from him. The temptation to look back over my shoulder is almost irresistible. I'm shaking now and when I hear a pop again I start. There's another pop. And another, followed by a long silence.

I hear him moving. Maybe I'll catch him off guard and be able to rush him soon. But to what point? He's got the gun and he probably weighs twice as much as I do, even if he is out of shape. Suddenly the lights go off. My heart beats like a son of a bitch. Should I make a run for it in the dark?

"Don't move. Just remember that I've still got the gun on you." I don't move. As my eyes adjust, I realize that I'm not in total darkness. A dim red light from behind casts my own faint shadow across the carpet and turns the fiberglass curtains pink.

"Turn back around." He stands before me, hugely naked, and erect, and still holding the gun. The red light tints his pale, hairless skin. The light comes from a lava lamp near the sofa, the grotesque blobs moving slowly through the viscous fluid. He wants me to suck him. I kneel and open my mouth. After the initial shock of flesh, it's not so bad. The repetitive movements are physically painless, their very familiarity almost soothing. Maybe he'll just come quickly, and then I can leave.

He doesn't come. After a time he orders me back to my feet. He squats down. He must want to suck me, and maybe while he's at it, I can get a hold on him or gouge his eyes or something. But no, he's going to watch while I jerk off.

"And this time get hard." Jesus Christ, how? Okay, just get a grip on yourself baby. Lots of times you've got it up for men who didn't attract you, even for men who repulsed you. But they weren't pointing a gun at me. Try to forget that. Use the familiar methods. I close my eyes, try to conjure beautiful bodies, lascivious scenes, but the image of his white, whale-like body is imprinted on my brain, obliterating all the others. Try getting off on yourself. I look down past a tanned, well-developed chest with big brown nipples jutting out, to a taut, powerfully muscled stomach, to a hand pumping a long cock. Gradually it rises.

"Go around behind me." He lifts himself on all fours, his ass sticking up in the air. Oh no, no way am I going to be able to fuck this man. My erection started falling, rapidly, the moment he spoke. "Now get on my back. And don't try anything, remember I've still got a gun."

"I don't understand. You want me to fuck you?"

"No. Straddle me." I lift a leg, then lower myself onto his back, wincing at the touch of the cold, enveloping flesh. "Now move back and forth like you're riding me."

"Like you're a horse?"

"That's right. Play with yourself as you're doing it,

but hold back, don't come too quickly." Considering the circumstances . . .

He begins bucking beneath me, at one point lifting my feet completely off the ground. I have to grab his shoulder to keep from falling off. I could sink my hands into his fat neck, tighten them around his throat. But "Remember I've got a gun," he said, and I remember. It's too risky.

"Yeah, ride 'em cowboy." I suppress a laugh. At least he can't see my face. Suddenly he stops bucking. The whole mass of flesh quivers beneath me and I hear a little grunt. Thank god, he's come.

"What are you doing?" I'm pulling on my socks.

"Can't I leave now?"

"That wasn't part of the deal, Mick. You agreed to spend the night with me." I know he's crazy now. *Part of the deal?*

"Fuck you, asshole. I'm not staying in this house a minute longer. Go ahead and shoot me if you want." He pulls the gun back out of his robe pocket. No, I didn't mean it. I say, look, what's the point of my staying any longer, we've already had sex? I say, look, I'm sorry, I shouldn't have yelled just now. I say I don't sleep well in other people's houses. I say my roommate's expecting me home, he's going to start getting worried. Then I threaten him with bodily harm, with the police, with freshly invented Mafia connections. I yell, I reason, I plead. Nothing moves him. He insists that I keep "my end of the bargain," then he'll pay me in the morning and I can leave. I know the part about the money is a lie, and maybe the part about letting me leave in the morning is a lie too.

How do I know that he won't hold me here indefinite-ly? Or kill me and bury me in his back yard?

No one knows where I am. Why didn't I keep trying to reach Max? I always call when I'm taking an outcall and give him the client's name, address, and phone number, or leave them on his answering machine, just in case "something should happen." Something has happened. But Max's line was busy tonight both times I phoned, and I was running late. Late. For this. The piece of paper on which I wrote the address here isn't even in my apartment, it's in the pocket of my jeans, over by the fireplace. Maybe when they're looking for me, if they ever look for me, they can trace the address from the indentations on the notepad, the way Cary Grant did in *North by Northwest.*

"Do you need to use the bathroom before we go to bed?"

"Yes." We go up the narrow staircase, me in front, he following with the gun at my back. Maybe I'll be able to lock the bathroom door and climb out the window, never mind that the room's on the second floor, I'll figure out something. But of course he stands in the doorway, watching me at the toilet.

"I thought you said you had to use the bathroom."

"I thought I did. I guess I'm just piss shy."

"Well, don't expect to be getting up in the middle of the night." For the first time there's an edge to his voice.

The small, pine-paneled bedroom has, I might have guessed, an oil portrait of a cowboy and, incredibly, bunk beds, narrow ones like children use. I'm to sleep on top. After I climb the little ladder, he pulls it away and leans it against the opposite wall. Did he buy the beds just for this purpose? How many others have been here before me? He switches off the overhead fixture, but the bright light of the moon shines through the sheer curtains of a large window. I watch from above as he climbs into the lower bunk, still wearing his plaid robe and still holding his pistol.

"Goodnight Mick." I will not say goodnight.

Is he awake or asleep? I must have been lying here for over an hour, cursing him, cursing myself, cursing the moonlight streaming through the window. And I've been plotting my escape. I might as well try now. I need to test him, make enough noise to get a response if he's awake but not enough to wake him if he's sleeping. I move in bed, as though I'm tossing in my sleep. My thrashings are tentative at first, then they become bolder. There's no response. I tap lightly on the side of the bed. Nothing. My second tap is louder. Again, nothing. Now on my stomach I inch toward the foot of the bed. Finally my entire body is crouched up in a ball near end rail. Now comes the hard part. I need to slowly lower myself down from the rail, making as little noise as possible and being careful not to kick the bottom bunk. The big risk will be in the final drop to the floor. If I stretch my body as much as I can the drop should only be a foot or two, and it helps that the floor is covered with shag carpet, but still there's no way of predicting how much these old floorboards will creak when I land. I lift my right leg over the edge of the bed, then my left. Clinging tightly to the rail I begin slowly lowering my torso. I hope the flimsy bed can hold my weight.

"Just remember that I've got a gun on you."

"My bladder's killing me."

"I warned you."

Much later. I hear a sibilant noise, like that made by an insect, perhaps a cicada. As it grows gradually louder, I recognize a human whisper. "Mick . . . Mick . . . Mick." I don't answer, don't move. Springs creak as he raises himself from his bunk. I close my eyes, pretend to be sleeping. I can feel him standing near me, watching me. After many minutes of this, I hear his footsteps move across the room, then down the uncarpeted hall. His footsteps stop; he must be in the bathroom. Quickly and silently I lower myself from the bunk. A light is shining from the open bathroom door. I've got to make a run for it. I'll sprint past the bathroom, catching him off guard—he won't be able to fire quickly enough—then down the stairway, which fortunately is not open—he won't be able to shoot from above, he'll have to come after me—then into the living room, pausing long enough to grab my clothes and car key, then out the front door to my car. If I can just make it to my car, I'll be okay. I take a deep breath. Now. That's when I see it. I can't believe him. The stupid fuck didn't even take his gun. It lies gleaming, like a dark jewel, against the pillow on the lower bunk. As my hand touches the cold metal, I hear his footsteps coming back down the hall. I try to remember what Odus told me about safety catches.

He sees me facing him with the gun, and his face is no longer expressionless. I fire. The bullet catches him right between the eyes. Then the huge lifeless body crashes to the floor.

Flight One

19

"YOU'VE GOT A lead ass," yells the manager of the Cherokee Strip Motel. He sits in a plastic lawn chair, poolside, drinking a Pabst Blue Ribbon beer.

"And your ass is grass," shouts back the boy in the water. "Watch," and the manager watches as the teenager, who is his son, executes a neat porpoise dive. The boy's underwater progress sends ripples across the small pool's entire surface, sets flecks of refracted sunlight into shimmering motion.

The manager finishes off his beer and places it beside two other empties on a wrought-iron table. He draws another from his sixpack.

"Neat, huh?" shouts the boy when he surfaces.

The manager grunts, smiles. "None of you kids can swim worth a good goddamn."

"Bull." The kid does a rapid crawl to pool's edge. Cupping his right hand, he sends a stream of water toward his father, but it just misses its target, hitting the concrete at his feet.

"Watch it, weasel," warns the man. The boy pulls himself from the water and shakes his thick dark hair, dog fashion, deliberately sprinkling his father. "God-dammit, weasel." The kid gives him the finger. "You want a drink?" The boy takes the Pabst from his father, shakes it. "Don't you dare," but the kid does dare. When he pulls the can's poptop a spray of foam spurts across his father's plaid shorts and his bare chest. The fight is on. Father and son yell curses at each other, chase each other around the pool, try to douse each other with beer. Inevitably they tumble into the water together. Some of the beer also lands in the pool; the foam floating across the water looks like ocean surf.

The two exchange a few more insults and mock punches as they dry themselves. They share the same tanned but heavily freckled skin, and they have similar bodies, well but not spectacularly proportioned, the son's shorter, thinner, less hairy, his father's in embryo. They gather up the empty beer cans and take turns pitching them across a patch of lawn. Each can lands with a clatter in a plastic trash holder near the coke machine.

"You want a beer?" the manager yells at me. "I've got one left."

"Sure."

"Someday," he leers as he hands me the warm can, "I'm going to *really* whip that little fucker's ass."

"Thanks."

"Fifteen going on sixteen. Some age," and the manager winks.

The sun has destroyed the beer's flavor, but the scent of chlorine filtered through dry, hot air is pungent, and as familiar as the scorching sun, the plastic lawn chairs, the roughhouse, and the not-quite-formed body of the teenage son.

When I was fifteen going on sixteen I swam most summer afternoons in the Beldon Municipal Pool in Beldon Park in the city and county of Beldon, Oklahoma. The pool honored Jerome T. Beldon, the park honored Miss Grace Beldon, and the city and county were named after their ancestors from three generations back, the ones who took the land from the Indians. Every morning that summer I waited anxiously near the telephone. If Sammy Lawe called, he'd pick me up in his gold and black '68 Mustang. I didn't get my driver's license until the following September, and Sammy, whose father bought him the car on his sixteenth birthday the previous February, was the only one I knew who was willing to drive the three miles out to the farm and take me to the pool. If Sammy didn't call by noon, I'd sometimes, although by no means always, and never without an agony of indecision, phone him. Often Mrs. Lawe or the Lawes' black maid Bertha told me that Sammy wasn't there, and since they never volunteered more information and I never asked for any, I'd spend the afternoon worrying about where Sammy was and with whom. If I reached him, he'd sometimes say, sure, he'd pick me up, but just as often he'd say, no, he wasn't going swimming today, or, sorry, he'd already told Bob Mason or Mike Sutterfield that he'd pick one of them up. The Mustang held four, of course, but it was understood that Sammy never took more than one of us to the pool. Bob didn't have his driver's license yet either, and although Mike did, his family only had one car, which his mother drove to her job every morning at the Top Heads Beauty Parlor, so the three of us were always in competition for a ride with Sammy. At least that's how I saw it, and it rankled that Bob and Mike lived in town, and so, unlike me, they *could* walk or bike to the pool, and, in fact, they usually did. The nights were different: Then all four of us would drag main in the Mustang or go to a party at the old James place by the river or drive into Tulsa to cruise the Ribbon.

I remember Sammy's blue and white striped trunks, a long straight nose (it was rumored that Mrs. Lawe's family had Indian blood), deep-set brown eyes, a stocky chest lightly feathered with sun-bleached down, a darker shadow of hair below his tan line. In the locker room we'd exchange curious and only minimally covert glances at each others' crotches as we slipped out of wet trunks into dry jeans. "It's bigger than this," Sammy said one day, catching me looking, "but you know how the water shrinks it." Teenage boys never showered at the Beldon Municipal Pool, only adults and children, which was why we usually smelled of chlorine in the summer. Nor did we use the pool on weekends, too crowded.

One Sunday morning in July Sammy and I ate some magic mushrooms, then went to the park and spent a couple of hours sitting high up in an oak tree, marveling at how *green* the grass and bushes stretched below us were, how *yellow* the roses. At one we drove to Tulsa to check out the action on Peoria, and when we got tired of that, we went out to Oral Roberts University. We liked to watch the eternal flame on top of the prayer tower when we were stoned, and we liked to provoke the university's security guards. After one of them with a doughboy face chased us away (his stated reason, the usual one, was that in jeans and bare chests we were "inappropriately dressed" to be on campus, "and you know it"), we headed home on Highway 64.

The Mustang hit eighty on the flat road, the breeze blew through the open windows and fanned out our long hair. As we passed the Beldon Funeral Parlor billboard, a couple of miles north of town, Sammy made the usual stale joke ("They've got the best lay-away plan in town"), at which we both laughed uncontrollably. When the KMOC disc jockey put on a favorite, "Mr. Tambourine Man," Sammy and I sang along. As our loud, harsh voices mingled with Bob Dylan's it was as though we were speaking to each other through the song's words, saying that we didn't want to go home, didn't want to leave each other, not yet. Sammy suggested that we pull off the highway and smoke a joint. We didn't need to stop to smoke a joint, of course, we never had before, but I agreed that we should. I was dizzy from the psilocybin and the heat and from anticipation. We headed down a familiar dirt road to a piece of unfenced land. The Mustang jumped as we turned into a field without slackening speed, and its motor growled as we ploughed through a head-high patch of Bermuda grass. Sammy stopped the car beneath a grove of sycamores and cut the engine.

Our fingers touched several times as we passed the joint. Sammy took in too much smoke and coughed. After he flicked the roach out of the window, neither of us spoke. I watched dust particles dance in the late afternoon sun and shadows from the trees play across the dashboard. Finally Sammy said he guessed we'd better get going. His hand reached for the keys in the ignition, stopped. His head turned to meet my gaze. A muscle in his left cheek twitched involuntarily. Our faces met in the center of the car. Sammy's mouth tasted of the sweet residue of marijuana, his upper lip of salt. I touched the smooth skin on the back of his neck, kneaded the muscle there. I felt an electric shock as his hand closed around my wrist. Then violently and almost simultaneously we reached for each other's cocks.

Sammy and I reached for each other's cocks a lot that summer and throughout the fall. We always made sure we were loaded on dope or alcohol first, and we never talked about what we did, either before, during, or after. We quit fooling around with each other in December, after Billy and Bobby Larsen showed up at the old James place unexpectedly one night and almost caught us sucking each other off on the floor of the deserted house. But Sammy and I remained good friends until I went away to Yale two years later. A year after that he was born again and married a girl from Stillwater.

Late afternoon shadows engulf the pool, turning its surface pearly green. I like the luxury of being alone in the cool water, I feel as though I'm in the middle of a Hockney painting. Except the sky's all wrong for a Hockney, and the lawn's not perfect enough. Patches of dead, yellowing grass interrupt the living areas of green, and the blue horizon is not flat and cloudless but sculpted and sprinkled with barely moving masses of white. I'd forgotten how close the sky seems to the earth here in Tulsa, you feel you could reach up and touch it. Completing a lap, I notice a movement behind the sliding glass door opposite me, as though someone had been watching me and dropped the curtain when I turned. I hope whoever it is doesn't plan to swim.

THE TULSA PHONE book has no listing for Odus Lynch, I checked when I arrived. But it shows a Judy Lynch at 631 Hawthore #6. I press the button to get an outside line. My finger hovers over the phone's numerals as I try and fail to grasp the point of what I'm doing. Perhaps there is no point. The dial tone grows progressively louder, more aggressive. I replace the receiver.

I light a cigarette and look again at the photograph above the television set. An attached caption reads HISTORIC WEST SERIES: SPIRIT DANCES OF THE MESCALERO APACHE. The sepia print, which is blurrily reproduced on thick cardboard, shows two figures bending toward the camera in stylized, "unnatural" poses. They've painted their chests and arms with intersecting dia-

mond patterns, and they wear elaborate skirts of
fringed leather and tall, identically carved head-
dresses. Dark masks completely obscure both faces.
When I first looked at the photograph I thought the
bleached-out background, ringed with scrawny
shrubs, was some sort of desert scene, but I now see
that the men are dancing in front of an institutional-
looking building of brick or perhaps of adobe. An
entrance and a second floor window are just visible,
both framed by Romanesque arches. And there's
something else I didn't see before: The photograph
contains a third figure. Behind the dancers and caught
at the very edge of the frame stands a white man in an
old-fashioned military uniform. The soldier watches
the Apache and because of the way his left arm is
angled, I think he's pointing a rifle at them. Impossible to know for certain, though, since the soldier's
right arm and the gun, if there is a gun, are blocked
from view by the dancer on the right. Exactly what's
going on here? I want to know when the scene took
place, but the caption gives no date. And it lists the
photographer as "unknown."

·—·—·—·21·—·—·—·

As I PULL into the Safeway parking lot and cut my lights, I meet a blue, 1964 Chevy convertible. Its driver has bleached her hair white, streaked it down the middle with black, and painted a green star on her left cheek. She smiles and waves as we pass. I wave back, and her throaty giggle carries across the thick night air.

Parking so that I can watch the crowd, I switch on the radio, and Dolly Parton asks me if I'm free tonight. Sure I am. Most of the FM stations here play only country and western now, and about half the boys milling around are wearing cowboy boots, which were taboo on the Ribbon just a few years ago. I get out of the car and, as is the custom, lean against the hood. Two teenage cowboys stare at me while I smoke a cigarette. When I nod, they approach, one tall and good-looking, the other shorter, with a small beer belly already beginning to jut across the top of his jeans. I learn that they're Brian and Mart and they learn that I'm from California and just passing through. Brian, the tall one, says that his brother was in California for awhile and wants to know if I ever heard of him, Len Qualls? I've never heard of Len. Brian says that's cool, Len lives in Amarillo now anyway, which is a real hick city. Len works in a bank and Brian doesn't even like to visit, the town's so fucking dead.

After we've shared a cigarette, Brian and Mart decide I'm not a cop. They're selling grass, acid, coke, and ludes, and they can probably get me some smack too, if that's what I want and if I've got the bucks. What I'm really interested in, I say, is some downers. Ludes are downers, Mart says. Undeniably, but, listen, I don't want to get fucked up tonight or get fucked, I just want to get some sleep, how about some reds? Mart and Brian exchange a look. Of suspicion? Disappointment? Brian asks why I want to sleep, I ought to party, enjoy the town. They can get me some good crystal or some bennies, either one. No thanks. Well, what the hell, Brian says, it's your funeral, Laurie's probably got some reds. They'll find her and send her over.

While I wait, I watch the bumper-to-bumper parade of cars down Peoria Street. A van with a shocking pink crucifix painted on its side slows as it passes, and half a dozen or so young girls stick their heads out of its windows. "We get high on Jesus!" they chant in unison, "We get high on Jesus! What do you get high on?" Cars behind them honk, and kids in the parking lot yell back curses and taunts. A boy who's been making out with his girlfriend jumps from the car next to me, a hard-on clearly outlined beneath his jeans. "You suck Jesus's cock too?" he shouts at the retreating van. "Jerry!" his girl protests, "get back in here." He reaches through the open door and pinches her bare breast. "Jerry!"

"You a cop?" I turn to face a small girl with blond, closely cropped hair and a round, freckled face. Laurie I presume. No, I'm not a cop, I say, I'm a fugitive from justice. Laurie says that's far out and smiles, revealing a mouthful of braces. She agrees to give me six reds, and I agree to give her the price she asks. A car honks at me as I leave the parking lot. I glance back to see Brian and Mart waving good-bye from a 1977 Mercedes 450 SL, the same year and model as Phillip's.

The man gets out of his car as I get out of mine. He's parked two spaces down from me, which probably means that his room is two doors down from mine. We nod at each other. After I unlock the door to my room, I glance back, and he's still standing beside his car, still looking in my direction. He's tall and broad-shouldered and obviously heavily muscled beneath his tight-fitting beige cotton suit, and his face is strong-boned, acne-scarred, handsome. But no thanks, I don't want to fuck a traveling salesman tonight, if that's what you are, and if that's what you have in mind. I've hardly slept for four days and nights, and I just want to get some rest. Truly.

22

MAN FOUND SLAIN IN BERKELEY

An East Bay man, Marcus J. Irving, was found shot to death in his home in the Berkeley hills yesterday. Police discovered Irving's nude, partially decomposed body at 3:00 P.M. when they responded to a call from the Haverford Office Supply Company in Oakland where Irving, 39, was employed as a shipping clerk.

Arriving at the rustic, isolated house where Irving lived alone, police found his body in an upstairs hallway. He had been shot in the head, and a .38 caliber pistol, presumed to be the murder weapon, lay near the body. According to homicide Inspector Conrad Ellsby, police have ruled out the possibility of suicide. "It definitely looks like murder," Ellsby said, although he added that police are still awaiting the final result of an autopsy.

Because of the decomposition of the body, police believe that Irving had been dead for several days, possibly as early as last Thursday. Police said Haverford Office Supply called them after Irving failed to appear at work on Friday and again on Monday and Tuesday and repeated attempts to reach him by phone were unsuccessful. "It just wasn't like him not to come to work," a company spokesman said yesterday, "he had an almost perfect attendance record."

Inspector Ellsby, who would not comment on details of the shooting, said that police had found "no known motive" for the murder but were pursuing several "promising leads." Other sources close to the investigation said that police found no signs of breaking and entering and therefore the killer was possibly someone known to Irving. They also said that police are seeking an as yet unidentified man for questioning, whom they believe may have been staying with Irving.

On learning of Irving's death, his neighbors in the quiet area expressed shock and apprehension. Some asked whether the motive for the murder might not be robbery and pointed out that a house just two doors down from the Irving property was robbed just last month. None of the neighbors remembered seeing Irving recently, but that was not unusual since his house was surrounded by a thick grove of trees. One neighbor who lives directly across the street from the scene of the murder did recall being awakened early Friday morning by a sound that police believe may have been a gunshot.

Talking with Irving's co-workers and neighbors, the picture that emerges is of a quiet and even reclusive man. A man who worked with Irving for five years at the Haverford Office Supply Company said yesterday, "I never got to know Mark really well, but he was a good guy. It just doesn't make sense. I can't think why anyone would want to kill him."

Police are still trying to locate Irving's next of kin.

TWO TIMES, THREE times, four times I read the front page story, my heart races, goose bumps sting my arms.

I reinsert the sports section, the entertainment section, the business section, and very carefully I fold the paper. When I return it to the periodical desk, a platinum blonde smiles at me, baring unnaturally white teeth. As I walk through the thickly carpeted, over-air-conditioned sterility of the library, the people around me seem to be department store dummies, silent, unmoving. I pray they won't come to life until I'm gone, and pray no one will be waiting at the elevator. No one is.

Stepping out into the ground-level parking lot, I flinch from the enveloping blast of heat. The interior of the Honda is also like a furnace, but I don't bother to roll down a window before I start the engine and pull out. I don't even bother to light a cigarette. Since Monday I've come daily to the glass-and-concrete Tulsa Civic Center to check out the San Francisco paper. Now there's finally the terrible relief of seeing the story in cold print.

But what can I make of the account's confusion? Take the matter of the "nude" body. When I left him several days, that night, when I left Marcus J. Irving, he was wearing a plaid bathrobe. Did someone arrive after me and remove the robe? But why? The "unidentified man" perhaps? Or is that supposed to be me? Maybe the paper is wrong, maybe a cop misinformed a reporter, or a reporter misinformed his desk. Maybe the newspaper simply made up the nudity, a case of pure sensationalism. Or could this be one of those deliberately misleading bits of information the police give out for the purpose of eventually trapping the murderer? (Detective: "So you say when you arrived that night Irving was dead. Describe what you saw." Suspect: "Well, he was in the upstairs hall naked." Detective: "You're lying. He wasn't naked, you read that in the goddamned newspaper. What else are you lying about, scumbag? You're lying about him being dead when you arrived, aren't you, aren't you?" Suspect: "I confess.")

What clues could the cops have, what "promising leads"? That night has run through my mind over and over again, a horror film in slow motion. What incriminating mistakes did I make?

I stand looking toward the fat man on his back thinking . . . nothing. Finally I move to the body. The hole in his forehead is surprisingly small, with only a thin trickle of blood oozing onto his right eyebrow. Although I know he's dead, I force myself to kneel down and reach through the blubbery flesh of his wrist for a pulse. There is no pulse.

I take a blue terrycloth hand towel from the bathroom and run it across the gun's smooth black surface. When I toss the gun to the floor, it skids across the marred wood and comes to rest near the body whose outstretched right hand seems to be reaching for it.

In the bathroom I wipe the towel rack, the toilet handle, the edge of the basin, in the bedroom the bedposts, the door frame, the little ladder. I take the Kodak he's left on the bedroom dresser, remove the roll of film he took of me, then wipe the camera too. Also on the dresser is a newspaper with my advertisement circled and a driver's license that gives me his name, age, height, weight. Loose change jingles to the floor when I grab the paper.

I run the towel along the banister as I descend, and downstairs I remove fingerprints from the kitchen counter and the bar stool. I even wipe surfaces I'm almost certain I didn't touch: a Danish modern end table near the fireplace, a plastic-upholstered reclining chair, the lava lamp.

I dress rapidly. I pull the strip of film from its plastic cartridge, exposing it to the light. Then I stuff it into a jacket pocket, I'll burn it when I get home. Newspaper and blue towel in hand, I head for the front door. Stop. What if he wrote down my name and number? I return to the kitchen and search the area near the telephone, being careful not to leave any more prints. I find pens and a notepad in a drawer beneath the phone, but the pad is blank.

I wipe the front door handle and the iron door knocker and listen for the sound of a passing car, or of movement from a nearby house. Only the deep moan of a distant foghorn breaks the silence.

I count three lighted windows and two glowing porchlamps as I drive down the narrow, winding road, but I meet no cars until I pull into traffic on Ashby.

"Late one tonight, huh, brother?" says the old black man at the bridge's tollbooth. The harsh neon lights show deep lines, cut like scars into his cheeks.

"Too late."

"Never too late." I'm overwhelmed with gratitude for the man's smile, and it's not until I'm halfway across the bay that I begin to shake. That's the point on the bridge where the city stretches out before you, majestic and beautiful and deeply romantic, its lights beckoning through the fog.

"HELLO, JUDY?"

"Yes."

"This is Cal."

"Yes?"

"Cal Lynch. I'm in Tulsa." Silence. "I'm sorry, is this the Judy Lynch—"

"Oh, *Cal,* my God, I recognize your voice, sure. I just didn't connect. . . . Where are you?"

"I'm in Tulsa."

"Really? How are you?"

"I'm doing okay. And you?"

"I'm fine." Silence.

"Is Odus there Judy?"

"Here?" Pause. "Oh, honey, it *has* been a long time. You wouldn't know about the divorce."

"No."

"Final over a year ago. Odus isn't in Tulsa anymore."

"I'm sorry."

"Thanks honey, but no need to be. I guess it was all for the best. Maybe."

"Would you know where I could reach Odus?"

"Oh sure. He's living back in Beldon now. I guess you wouldn't know about that either. He built a new house on the farm, real showplace. I might have stayed if he'd built that house when I was with him, but he didn't. But he sure built it quick enough for that floozy. But to tell you the truth, Cal, we'd moved back to Beldon, right after your mother died, and I just couldn't stand the place. I really think that's the real reason I left him. I mean, I could probably have dealt with that floozy if it hadn't been for that damn little town. Nothing ever changes there. You were smart to get away from it when you did."

"Do you have Odus's number?"

"Sure, you ought to give him a call. It's 238-4621."

"The same number we always had."

"What? Oh, yes, that's right. The same old number. As I said, nothing ever changes in that little town. I'm sure he'll be glad to hear from you."

"I don't know."

"I know you two went through some pretty rough

times together, but forgive and forget. Hell, *I've* even forgiven Odus. Almost. What's the point of bitterness? And I've met someone myself. Bobby's a little younger than me, Cal, but why not? You ought to come over for a beer some night and meet him, I think you two would get along. And you could see the kids." Pause. "What are you doing with yourself these days, Cal?"

"Modeling."

"No kidding? Clothes? Sounds glamorous. You must be as good-looking as ever then. Still a bachelor?"

"Yes."

"So what are you doing, Cal? In Oklahoma, I mean?"

"Just here for a visit. Vacation I guess."

"Funny place for a vacation, not to be rude. You're not going to start anything up with Odus again, are you? Not that it's any of my business. But just between you and me, I do think you got a raw deal. I can see that better now, after the way Odus treated me. Although I have to say that I came out all right, financially speaking."

"Still teaching school?"

"Yes, fifth grade now. I think the last time I saw you I was still in third. How many years has it been?"

"Judy, thanks for the number. And I'm sorry about you and Odus."

"Yes, it has been a long time. Listen, Cal, I really did mean that about coming over for a beer. How long are you going to be in town?"

"I'm not sure yet."

"Well, give Odus a call. Maybe we can all have a big reunion, wouldn't that be a hoot? You call me back if you want to come over, any time. Bobby and I'll take you out to the club."

"Thanks Judy. Good-bye now."

"Bye honey."

ON SCREEN: THE tanned face of Jimmy Lee Campbell, tanned and jowly, with sparkling teeth, large brown eyes, and wavy gray hair that rises to a distinguished widow's peak. Jimmy Lee invites everyone to come on out to the fairground this weekend and join him for his annual "Christians Against Communists" rally. With our help the battle *can* be won.

My Aunt Em worried a lot about communism too. She gave money to George Wallace's presidential campaign and was, quite possibly, a follower of Jimmy Lee's. I remember this about Aunt Em: She worked for thirty years behind the lingerie counter at Brown's Department Store, she raised violets and baked oatmeal cookies with gnarled, arthritic hands, and the night before I went away to college she came over and warned me not to get mixed up with the

Students for a Democratic Society. They were communist infiltrators who were trying to overthrow the government, and Aunt Em said that although she knew I was smart, she also knew that they preyed on young, idealistic kids like me. Actually during my years in New Haven, my friends and I were mainly concerned with getting into law school or med school or architectural school or whatever, and also with getting laid and getting stoned. Idealism was not our problem. The Students for a Democratic Society were already fading, and their contemporaries, the Black Panthers, whose brief but notorious Yale connection Aunt Em had somehow missed, would soon be either dead or in jail or capitalist entrepreneurs. But Aunt Em nodded gravely when I assured her that I'd be on my guard, and then she gave me a hundred dollars and said she knew I'd make the family proud.

And I remember this about Jimmy Lee Campbell: that he survived a scandal. Several years ago, the summer I lived in Tulsa with Susan, two of Jimmy Lee's young and, as it turned out, specially favored disciples were married. Reverend Campbell himself performed the ceremony. That night in bed, before giving herself to her husband, the bride felt compelled to confess her sin to him. She was not, she said, a virgin. She had, in fact, had intercourse on dozens of occasions. Naturally, the young man wanted to know with whom. With Jimmy Lee Campbell, she said. At which point her groom confessed that he also had had intercourse on dozens of occasions. Also with Jimmy Lee Campbell.

For whatever private reasons—of shame, of revenge, of Christian duty—the newlyweds decided to go public with their guilty knowledge, decided to "expose" the Reverend Jimmy Lee. Their scrubbed and very photogenic faces, an image of wronged innocence, appeared nightly on the local news, dominated the front pages of the Tulsa papers for days. *Time* and *Newsweek* covered their allegations, and *60 Minutes* considered doing a profile of the couple.

For an entire month, as the media storm swirled around him and as his followers divided into vehemently pro- and anti-Campbell factions, Jimmy Lee remained in seclusion. Then one Sunday the Reverend Campbell stepped into the pulpit of his showplace God and Country Chapel to answer his enemies. To the television cameras and to what was left of his flock, Jimmy Lee said this: The young couple was to be honored, not scorned, for the newlyweds were only doing their duty to God. Their accusations were true, and now he, Jimmy Lee Campbell, came before the world as a wretched sinner. The congregation gasped. Jimmy Lee explained that a year ago Satan himself had entered into him, had taken possession of his body and his soul, had caused him to commit adultery, sodomy, and a host of other sins. In brief, the devil made him do it. Employing all of his very considerable rhetorical gifts, Jimmy Lee described, in dramatic and graphic detail, his struggle with the forces of evil. He told the congregation that he had finally succeeded in exorcising Satan from his soul, but he could now say, from painful firsthand experience, that Satan could enter any of us at any time, that the price we pay for salvation is eternal vigilance. In other words, Jimmy Lee fashioned a cautionary fable. And he also pointed out that in choosing to possess him, Satan had an ulterior motive. Not only did he want to make Jimmy Lee perform abominations, he also wanted to bring disgrace upon a chosen messenger of God.

The tide turned. Nearly everyone in the God and Country Chapel and many watching at home on TV were moved to tears by the battle between good and evil Jimmy Lee so passionately described; no one wanted to be taken in by the dirty trick Satan had so obviously played on Reverend Campbell. By confessing his sins, Jimmy Lee succeeded in bringing back the straying members of his flock. In the end, he retained his followers, his donations, his annual crusade against communism, and his four-million-dollar highrise in the center of Tulsa. After all, the devil made him do it.

Did the devil make me do it? I think not. There is this ugly fact: I did not have to kill the man. He was a liar and a cheat, yes, he was stupid and ugly and brutal. He pulled a gun on me, he threatened to shoot me, and, in effect, he raped me. But once I had that gun I was in control. I could have escaped. I could even have scared the shit out of him and then escaped. I did not have to kill the man. However, there is also this ugly fact: For that moment I wanted to kill him. Two facts really: I wanted to kill him and I did.

It would be convenient if I could, like Jimmy Lee Campbell, confess my sin and be saved. Unfortunately I do not believe in God.

·—·—· 25 ·—·—·

AN ANIMAL INSTINCT tells you when someone is in your presence, an instinct independent of both sight and sound. My eyes are closed; and what I hear is Kris Kristofferson's gravelly lament for lost innocence on the radio and the distant hum of highway traffic, certainly neither footsteps nor any other sound of nearby human movement. Yet I know someone is with me.

Splintered rays from the noonday sun shoot into my eyes; painful, they momentarily blind me. Then in fragments, as though between the flashes of a strobe, I see him. A man stands directly across the pool from me, looking in my direction. He's tall. He's broad-shouldered. He's the same man who was outside my door a couple of nights ago. He wore a beige, tight-fitting cotton suit then, and he wears the same suit now, with a bright green Polo shirt. He's staring at me. But is he? A camera hides his face. He's taking a picture.

The man stands at least a hundred feet from me, but perhaps he's using a telephoto lens, I can't tell. He lowers the camera from his face, but the sun's behind him, shining into my eyes, and I can't read his expression. Maybe he gets his kicks out of taking pictures of men in skimpy bathing suits and has albums at home filled with beefcake. Maybe the photograph is just a ploy, an excuse to introduce himself to me. I thought he was trying to pick me up the other night, and this is probably another attempt, in a minute he'll come over and begin his come-on. ("I hope you don't mind my taking your picture, it's my hobby, you know.")

The man lifts the camera to his eyes again. I reach for the sunglasses lying on a wrought-iron table beside me, so that I can try to see his face more clearly when he completes this shot. But just as I fit the stems of the glasses over my ears, the man turns, and his tan-suited backside disappears into what is presumably his room. A door slides shut, its glass surface reflecting the pool and patio and obscuring the room's interior. I put the sunglasses back on the table and light a cigarette. I close my eyes. I have the distinct feeling that the man's still watching me, spying on me from behind the obscuring glass door.

What if he is *really* spying on me? I suddenly turn chill beneath the hot sun, shudder. What if they've somehow connected me to the murder in Berkeley and the man has me under surveillance? Since that initial article last Thursday, the San Francisco paper has had nothing more on the killing of Marcus Irving, and in this case I suppose that no news could be either good news or bad. But even if they have connected me to the murder—how?—it's simply not possible that they've found me here. No one in California even knows that I'm in Tulsa, I've covered my trail, covered my ass. And, of course, if the man were a cop or an FBI agent he wouldn't be snapping pictures of me in broad daylight. Would he? No, this is not the time to turn paranoid.

I put out my cigarette and immediately light another one.

26

I'M COMING OUT of the auditorium at the university when someone behind me calls my name. I stifle an impulse to keep walking straight ahead, to *run*. There's no one in the world I want to see tonight; the idea of having a conversation with anyone seems, just now, impossible. Nevertheless, I stop. When I turn I see a man with close-cropped black hair and a matching beard hurrying toward me through the crowd. At his side a woman, taller than he, also with close-cropped, dark hair, and dressed in an odd, Japanese-style tunic, tries to keep pace.

"Cal Lynch. Cal." Mike Sutterfield smiles, shakes

his head in mock wonder, clasps his hands over mine. Caught.

"Mike."

"I'm Lynda," the woman says. I look over Mike's shoulder into her eyes, which are small and very, very black. Mike explains that I'm a friend from Beldon who's been away in New York.

"Did you like the movie?" Lynda asks, still holding my gaze. A grainy sixteen-millimeter print of Fritz Lang's *Metropolis*.

"Yes, especially the robot Maria." Slowly Lynda closes her left eye, imitating the robot's lewd wink.

"Quite a paradigm," she says. "All the workers live underground, and the upper classes live above them. Someone should write a song about it."

"Called 'The New Metropolis,'" Mike suggests.

"Or 'The Subways of New York,'" I say.

"Right," Lynda says, "either title would do."

The hair is shorter and the beard is new, and Mike has finally lost his adolescent pudginess. In fact, he's almost skinny now, and newly muscled, wiry. My longtime and then long-lost buddy. When we were kids Mike had two pet rabbits, Mr. Rabbit and Mr. Fox, that I used to help him feed in his back yard after school. We also pitched baseballs in that yard and buried girlie magazines wrapped in plastic in the sandy soil beneath a weeping willow. Mike was overweight then, and then and later he had the not especially enviable reputation of being the smartest kid in class. He was the spelling champion when we were in the eighth grade, and he was the valedictorian when we were seniors. He was, for a time, my shadow rival for Sammy's affection, and several years after that he met Susan and became her defender and hence my accuser. ("Maybe I shouldn't butt in," I remember him telling me that summer, his voice shaking with anger, "but you're making that girl miserable. Goddamn miserable.")

Now Mike teaches freshman English at Tulsa University, where he's writing ("in theory at least") his doctoral dissertation on John Berryman's "Dream Songs." He also plays bass guitar in a new wave rock band called Empty Space and writes most of the group's songs. At this point, the band gets occasional local gigs, and they're trying to get the money together to make a dynamite demo tape.

Mike and gimlet-eyed Lynda met on New Year's Eve a year and a half ago at a Talking Heads concert in Dallas. Since she came to Tulsa to be with Mike ("It was easier for me to move," she says, somewhat defensively, "Mike's more *rooted* than I"), Lynda has been writing fashion copy and doing layouts for the advertising department of Hansen's Emporiums. For the last six months the two of them have been living ("This should interest you, Cal," Mike says. "Cal studied architecture," he explains to Lynda) in the servants' quarters of the only house that Frank Lloyd Wright built in Tulsa. A friend of Mike's, who's a real estate agent, is having a hard time selling the place, and in exchange for the butler's cottage and a small salary Mike and Lynda look after the big, empty main house and keep the grass cut.

"You have to come out and see the monster," Mike says.

"Yes," Lynda agrees, after a slight but perceptible pause, "talk about visionary. Fritz Lang's set designer had nothing on Frank Lloyd Wright."

"I don't know, I'm not sure how long I'll be in town." Of course I won't visit them. We're on our third pitcher of beer in a dark, noisy student hangout near the university, and I'm drunk. Mike's obvious, if perhaps overly histrionic, pleasure in finding me after . . . what? five years? . . . shamed me into accompanying him and Lynda here. Now, probably because of my alcoholic haze, I can't tell whether I'm enjoying talking to them or whether I'm only pretending to enjoy myself. I suppose I would have had to see someone sooner or later, I couldn't remain mute and antisocial forever. It might as well have been sooner and it might as well have been Mike. But of course I won't visit them.

In response to Mike's and Lynda's questions and in exchange for an updated précis of his life and an abridged account of hers, I've told them that I've been living in Los Angeles for two years, that I've been acting in theater and doing some TV commercials ("No, nothing you would have seen, just local stuff, used cars and furniture sales"), and that I'm on my way back to LA after visiting a friend in New York. I've also lied about where I'm staying in Tulsa, just in case they try to get in touch again. And I lie now when Mike asks me how Odus is. Odus is just fine, I say, implying that I've seen him, which I haven't. I quickly ask if anyone wants to get another pitcher of beer.

"Have you heard the latest about Sammy?" Mike asks. "Shit." He's miscalculated the aim from pitcher to glass and splattered beer across the redwood table-top.

"No."

"Well, you know he was born again? And now, you

won't believe this, he's become an evangelist. A *successful* evangelist. He's always giving crusades and revival meetings and getting his picture in the paper. They carry some of his sermons on cable. He's the handsome one," Mike says to Lynda.

"I know who he is. It seems like everyone from that little high school group of yours went into some branch of show business." Is there an edge to her voice?

"Yeah, I suppose you could say we did. Except Bob Mason. Barracuda Bob. The last I heard of Bob he was working in a factory in Galveston, organizing workers. He's supposed to be a communist."

"Isn't that a bit passé?" Lynda asks. There definitely is an edge to her voice. She's probably tired of all the nostalgia. So am I. I have a sudden urge to lean across the table and say, *sotto voce,* "I'm a murderer, you know."

"Imagine," Mike continues, "Bob's family has all that money, and he's working in a factory. Hell, I'm the one who's supposed to be the proletarian." Mike's father was a janitor, his mother a beautician. "Of course you know how people are in Beldon, Cal. To them everyone's a communist, it's probably not even true."

"Probably not." But possibly so. Which would mean two converts, Barracuda Bob to Marxism, Sammy to religion, two proselytizers, an "organizer" and a preacher. I wonder if Sammy, like Saint Augustine and like Jimmy Lee Campbell, uses his past sins to illustrate his evangelical message, peppers his sermons with the abominations he used to perform? For example, fucking me.

"What?" I've missed Mike's question.

"Are you still in touch with Susan?" When I look into Mike's face, it's bleary-eyed and curious, not malicious.

"No."

"I just wondered."

"Listen guys," Lynda says, "I've got to get up and go to work in the morning. Who's Susan?"

"One of Cal's ex's."

"I thought you were gay?"

"Susan was a long time ago."

"You should meet Tom Tree." Tom Tree, Mike explains, is the lead singer of Empty Space.

I WALK SLOWLY through a silent landscape. Ancient oaks surround me, their branches tower overhead, partially bare and partially clustered with dry leaves that filter the pale, yellowish light of late afternoon. Under my feet are more leaves, a soft carpet of gray and brown, ocher and faded green. Mist rising from the ground envelops the trees and seems to suspend the world in time. A time out of mind, a place both faraway and familiar. Yes, I've been here before. As I trudge ahead, I'm aware that my destination, although unknown to me, is somehow preordained, fated. I'm anxious and exhilarated, as though at the beginning of a great but potentially dangerous adventure. The icy air stings my throat and lungs before coming out of my mouth as swirling clouds of steam.

In the far distance a house appears amidst the trees. As I draw closer, I recognize the outlines of Aunt Em's big Victorian. Except the house is now shorn of its wire fence, its neatly-tended flower beds, its neighbors; and it's no longer white. Its autumnal noncolor blends into the forest, which has surrounded, engulfed, claimed it. Of course, Aunt Em's is where I'm going!

Suddenly, unaware of any transition from the outdoors, I'm standing in the room at the back of the house that Aunt Em always called her "dining room." In fact, the room did have a big, ugly mahogany dining table, but the only time it was ever used was for family dinners on Thanksgiving. The rest of the year the table and its matching chairs were pushed into a corner to make room for Aunt Em's real life. For this was where she received her many visitors, where she played canasta on hot summer nights at a card table set up near the screened porch, where she watched television from an old velvet davenport, and where she tended the violets massed beneath the west windows. Now the room is abandoned and dilapidated, seemingly at the mercy of the elements. The furniture is gone, the flowered wallpaper is waterstreaked and tattered, the floor is covered with leaves. The room is also much larger than I remembered, enormous really, as though it had expanded to take over the entire ground floor of the house. When did I become aware of the man standing at the far end of the room? It seems as though I've always known he was there, even when I was walking through the forest, even before the house came into view.

But wait, look over there. A piece of Aunt Em's furniture is still here. The antique mahogany sideboard is standing where it always stood, against the wall beside the big sliding doors to the living room. And sitting on the sideboard's top, in exactly the place where they always sat, are the chickens, two red and white and yellow ceramic chickens. Aunt Em filled the hollow center of the larger chicken with wax fruit, the center of the smaller one with loose change. Moving closer now, I see that the sideboard is covered with dust and mildew and that the chickens are empty. I reach to pet the larger chicken, but my hand stops in mid-air when I realize that she's been mutilated. Her right wing is broken off and both of her yellow claws are missing. I drop to my knees and search frantically for the missing pieces among the leaves. Hot tears sting my eyes, I'm filled with an enormous despair.

I'm walking through the forest toward the man who stands at the far end of the dining room. The walls between indoors and out have vanished, the room has become an extension of the forest. The man wears a floppy black hat and a tan trenchcoat, whose big collar he's pulled up as protection against the storm. For a strong wind blows now, whistling through the trees, and a heavy rain falls. Sodden leaves squish beneath my feet and icy rain slaps my face as I move closer, closer. I've been tracking the man; now he's in range. I stop, catch my breath, and lift the rifle that I've been carrying all along. As I sight along the barrel

I see him take a drag from a cigarette, then toss it to the ground. I cock the gun. Time stops as the man and I face each other, both immobile in the storm. Then I pull the trigger, and it's at exactly that moment that I realize he's my father. Oh Daddy, my Daddy. Daddy.

There's that momentary flash of panic, which seems to last forever, when you wake up and don't know where you are, you're trapped in darkness. In a cheap hotel room in Barcelona? In the apartment in Gramercy Park? In California? In Beldon? I make out a faint glow on my left, yes, where light shines through . . . what? Diamond-patterned drapes drawn across a wall of windows. Silhouetted against the glow are a square easy chair beside a small table holding a big round lamp. Of course, I'm in a motel room in Tulsa. I've come here to get away, I'm hiding here; and I'm freezing. Glancing down, I realize that I'm uncovered, and I pull up sheet, blanket, and quilted bedspread to protect me from the chill of an overactive air conditioner. I light a cigarette and watch its orange tip glow in the dark as the narrative comes back to me in fragments, the narrative and its final horror.

Well, what son has not dreamed of killing his father?

This is only the latest in a series of such dreams I've had over the years, variations on a theme. Examples: I dreamed I pushed my father out of an airplane high above the mountains of Colorado; I dreamed I rescued a stranger from quicksand, while nearby my father slowly sank into the mud; I dreamed I ran down my father with a car in front of a gaudy Moslem temple; I dreamed I pulled a cord that sent my father floating into the sky in a silver balloon that never returned to earth. And now I've dreamed that I hunted my father as prey. I'm not much given to the interpretation of dreams, but the connection between this latest nightmare and what I did last week in Berkeley is, I suppose, a bit too obvious to miss.

I don't need to kill my father, of course; he's already dead, has been dead for over a decade. He had a massive and fatal coronary in the middle of Belimore's feed store when I was fifteen. Seven years after that my mother died of lung cancer, although she never smoked a cigarette in her life. For several years now I've told anyone who asked that I'm an orphan. That's true enough in a literal sense, but I realize that "orphan," as that term is commonly understood, does not really apply to me.

ON JUNE 29 the *San Francisco Chronicle* runs a dark, underexposed photograph of a young man on page eight. The scowling face, beefy and rather babyish, is surrounded by a mass of curly blond hair. The eyes, though, appear to be dark, they're brown perhaps, or black; and they're small and deep-set. A caption identifies the man as Raymond Bell, and beside the photograph is this story:

MAN SOUGHT IN
EAST BAY SLAYING

Berkeley police announced yesterday that they are now seeking Raymond Bell of San Francisco for questioning in connection with the murder of Marcus J. Irving in Berkeley two weeks ago. Irving, 39, was found shot to death at his home in an isolated area of the Berkeley hills last Wednesday afternoon. According to homicide Inspector Conrad Ellsby, Irving's partially clad body was at that time badly decomposed, and police now believe he probably died sometime during the early hours of the previous Friday.

Ellsby declined to say whether police consider Bell, 19, a suspect in the case. Witnesses have told police that Bell and Irving left a Tenderloin bar, The Cat's Meow, together around midnight on June 12, the night before Irving is believed to have been killed. Irving, who was employed by the Haverford Office Supply Company in Oakland, did not appear for work that Friday, and police say Bell may have been the last person to see him alive. Raymond Bell, also known as "Buddy," was apparently unemployed, and is described as around five-feet-eight, of medium build, with blond hair and brown eyes.

Bell has not been seen since last Friday when he checked out of a residential hotel at 531 Turk where he had been living for three months. Bell told one resident there that he planned to leave town and return to his native South Carolina. According to Ellsby, police are now in touch with South Carolina authorities.

Whatever else he may be, it's obvious that Raymond Bell, also known as "Buddy," is a hustler, given his age, his address, and the fact that he left the Cat's Meow with Marcus Irving. The bar is known as a place where street trade and middle-aged johns connect. Did Buddy become one of Irving's victims after they left the bar that night, was he also forced to have sex at gunpoint? Could the photograph of Buddy in the newspaper actually be one that Irving took, which the police found later in the Berkeley house?

Where is Buddy now? Hiding out in a motel room? Perhaps in his "native South Carolina"? Why did he leave town? For a split second I consider the possibility that maybe Buddy did kill Irving, that it wasn't me after all. For a split second. If the police do find Buddy, and if they somehow manage to convict him of Irving's murder, will I step forward to save an innocent man?

While the June 29 story raises a lot of new and unwelcome questions, it at least seems to answer one old question. The initial newspaper account of Irving's murder told of police discovering his "nude" body, but when I left him that night Irving was wearing a flannel bathrobe. That tallies with the more recent "partially clad" description, so the first account may—must—have been wrong.

However, the new story fails to answer another

question that's been gnawing at me since I read that first article. "Authorities" were at that time trying to locate Irving's "next of kin." Did they? I've been fervently hoping that he had no next of kin.

IT WAS WHILE I was watching *The Match Game* this morning that I remembered reading a detective novel in which the police caught a mass murderer by lifting an impression of his tire tracks from the field in which they found one of the women he raped and strangled.

At the Sears store in the Rolling Hills Mall I make a point of telling the clerk that I'm planning to drive to Alaska soon, in case he questions me about why I'm getting rid of relatively new tires. But the clerk is young and eager to please in his jacket and tie and heavily starched white shirt, and he shows no interest in the state of my tires. He's only interested in selling me some new ones, and he quickly convinces me to buy four medium-duty Uniroyals for $274.34, including tax. He warns that a mechanic won't be able to get to my car for at least an hour, and I say that's okay, I'll just take a walk around the mall and try to find a mosquito net for my trip. The clerk looks momentarily nonplussed, but he recovers and suggests that I try Byer's Sporting Goods. We settle the bill. I pay for the tires, as I pay for everything now, with cash. I withdrew three thousand dollars from my San Francisco bank before I left: I don't want to leave a paper trail.

I wonder whether I ought to have the clerk put the used tires in the back seat of the Honda. I could drive out and throw them into the Cimarron River. But the shop will probably resell the tires either to someone looking for a bargain or to a scrap dealer, so there's perhaps no need to worry about them eventually being traced to me, no need to sink them in the Cimarron.

Since I was a kid, I've loved sitting beside the fountain in the center of the mall. The air, heavily filtered, almost aqueous, makes you feel like you've been removed from ordinary life, transported to some rarefied, technological Eden. The floors are made of glazed bricks and the neutral-toned walls and ceiling are of raked plaster. In the center of the fountain as big as a swimming pool stands an island of tall podocarpus trees, whose delicate, spear-shaped leaves reach toward an enormous, soji-like skylight. Rushing water drowns out the roar of the crowd, as does the Muzak, which is so rhythmically attenuated that it becomes almost Japanese in its balance and serenity. Indeed, the whole effect here is oddly Oriental, of nature becalmed, abstracted, perhaps betrayed.

Of course, this is America. The heart of America, some would say. One of America's many hearts. A life-sized, mechanical Uncle Sam in front of the nearest shop tells you that, doesn't it? The shop is called the Family Jewels, and the stripes of Uncle Sam's pants are alternating rows of glass rubies and dime-store pearls. His top hat is banded by rhinestones. I've never been inside the Family Jewels, but I still own a blue blazer that my mother and I purchased at the Varsity Shop, which is just around the corner. We bought the blazer for me to wear to the junior-senior prom.

"I should never have let him know I didn't need that wheelchair anymore," says a gray-haired lady sitting on the bench to my left.

"No," agrees her companion, also a handsome elderly lady, who has tinted her hair lavender. Half a dozen or so packages of the women's purchases sit beside them on the bench, and a pile of their half-smoked cigarette butts lies at their feet.

Across from me a young black woman lifts a small child, presumably her son, and suspends him over the rim of the fountain. Slowly she lowers the boy until his bare feet are completely immersed in the bubbling water. I can't tell whether his muffled squeals are from pleasure or from fear.

"No," says the gray-haired woman, "the day he found out I didn't need that wheelchair anymore was the day he walked out."

The black woman sits her son on the fountain's stone rim, and a girl child, presumably the woman's daughter, scrambles into her arms. Again, the woman lowers a child into the fountain. A couple of older girls stand nearby watching, they're ten or eleven perhaps and not black. They clap when the little girl's feet finally enter the water. The mother rewards them with a wan smile, the daughter sticks out her tongue.

"I saw her the other day at Robert Hall's," says the woman with lavender hair. "I didn't want to tell you this, Wilma, but I think she's had a face lift."

"Damn her."

I glimpse a familiar profile through the podocarpus foliage. Standing across the mall from me, looking into a window that displays a book by a Watergate criminal, is that man from the motel. George. Today he's wearing a blue Polo shirt with his tan cotton suit, and he's eating a doughnut. Fortunately he hasn't looked in my direction yet. I don't want to run into him again. Yesterday morning he sat down next to me at the counter in the motel coffee shop and tried to strike up a conversation. I answered all of his queries with monosyllables and refused to ask any questions of my own. Undaunted, George volunteered the information that he's from Saint Louis, that he is, as I guessed, a salesman (of hospital equipment), and that he spends a lot of time in Tulsa, since it's part of his territory. George did not volunteer an explanation of why he was photographing me. His voice was deep, with a faint Irish lilt, and up close he turned out to be very handsome indeed, and older than I thought, his dark rugged face both threatened and enhanced by deep weather lines and old acne scars. When George invited me to drive downtown to the Y with him to work out, I declined. "Saint Theresa not interested," I said to myself as I left the coffee shop, remembering a line from a Gertrude Stein-Virgil Thomson opera that Michael Worth used to play a lot. Now I rise to move away before George spots me here. Saint Theresa still not interested.

* * *

You're doing something perfectly normal. You're walking down the street, for example, or, just now, down a crowded aisle of the Humpty Dumpty supermarket. Like everyone else, you put one foot before the other. You scan the shelves, smell oranges and overripe bananas, accidentally jostle a woman's cart. Then suddenly, with no apparent catalyst needed, you remember that you're a murderer. A murderer looking for a tube of Prell. The ground shifts. Assumptions that you've always taken for granted vanish at these moments of remembering. The continuity between your experience and the experience of those around you has been broken; it now strikes you as truly amazing that you're still capable of sitting beside a fountain at all, or of casually strolling through a mall, or of shopping in a supermarket. There's an unbridgeable gap between what you've done and what these people around you have done, or, more precisely, what they haven't done. It's as though you've taken a drug whose horrific and irreversible effects you can't possibly explain, let alone justify, to anyone who hasn't taken the same hallucinogen. You know something that others will never know. Is it possible that you even feel a certain superiority, a sense of emotional one-upmanship? Yes, perhaps. But you'd give anything not to have this knowledge. If you could return to the old innocence, you'd gladly sell your soul. If, that is, you hadn't already sold it.

·—·—·— 30 ·—·—·—

"JUDY SAID YOU called. She didn't know where you were staying, or I would have called you."

"Would you?"

Odus looks back over his shoulder, studies my face, then turns away without answering my question. I imagined (or was it hoped?) that my brother would have lost his looks. I imagined that he, like a lot of men in their mid-thirties with ex-wives, kids, and bills to pay, would have developed a paunch, or gained too much weight, or gone gray or bald. I imagined a face coarsened and thickened with age.

In fact Odus looks terrific. He stands on a ladder, his back toward me, and the light from half-opened venetian blinds catches sun-bleached highlights in his hair, which is still thick and brown and curly. A tight T-shirt emphasizes his football shoulders, and, as he rolls terra-cotta paint onto a wall, the muscles and sinews and veins of his raised forearm stand out as vividly as those in an anatomical drawing.

Odus looks terrific, but he's unhappy. That's why

he's painting his bedroom. Last week Cyndy, the woman he's been living with for over two years, left him. She quit her job and went to New Orleans. When Cyndy had first moved in with him, Odus tells me, she'd insisted that their bedroom be pink. A nurse, she'd countered Odus's objections to such a feminine shade by citing a hospital study which showed that terminal patients found pink the most soothing of colors.

"Soothing hell. Drives me crazy. Always did." So the bedroom where Odus now sleeps alone has a pale pink wall, two terra-cotta walls, and a transitional fourth on which Odus aggressively and I assume symbolically rolls paint. Yet as he blots out his life with Cyndy, he laments her leaving. His lamentations are familiar, and his mixture of wounded pride, bewilderment, and anger is the same combination I remember seeing the first time he and Judy separated. Constantly (and unfortunately for him carelessly) promiscuous, Odus can't understand why his women object so passionately when they find out about his affairs. *"Casual* affairs," he emphasizes. "I mean I can *understand,* but Christ, she didn't have to duck tail and split. Screw her. . . . You think I ought to paint the ceiling this color too, or just leave it white?" Is Odus making a conscious attempt to solicit my "professional" opinion? I've told him that I'm working for a firm in San Francisco that does interior architecture.

"White." The living room of Odus's new house has exposed redwood beams, but the ceilings of the other seven rooms are made of white "acoustical" plaster that looks like cottage cheese. The redwood and glass house stands on the crest of a low hill and overlooks the old dirt access road, which Odus has paved with asphalt, and the old wells, several of which are still pumping oil and money. Odus's new house stands, in fact, exactly where the old gray farmhouse stood, the one in which he and I grew up. When I arrived Odus gave me a tour of the new place, and as I walked through the cool, silent rooms, it occurred to me that I should be reacting in some way to my brother's destruction of our childhood home. With regret perhaps, or nostalgia, or anger at Odus for tearing it down. I felt nothing. On the other hand, Odus's suburban dream doesn't interest me. Nor, I think, now that a certain initial curiosity has been satisfied, does my brother interest me.

He climbs down the ladder and takes another Coors from the top of a newspaper-covered dresser. It's his fourth since I've been here. He throws back his head and chug-a-lugs half a bottle.

"You're getting your checks, aren't you? No problem with those is there, Cal?"

"No problem." Odus looks at me searchingly. He's still trying to figure out why I'm here, he doesn't understand why I've turned up after four years. I don't understand why either.

"You know, I've been putting most of your dividends into a real estate holding company. We're the ones doing that new development south of town. River Bend. You should take a look at it before you leave. Twenty-five units. Condos that are already beginning to sell like hotcakes. Mainly to commuters from Tulsa . . . I know you don't like how things were set up, but what I'm saying is that I'm trying to do well by you, and I am. You're going to have quite a pile when you turn thirty-five."

"If I live that long."

"What?"

"I'll probably be dead before I'm thirty-five."

"Christ, I can't believe you're that much of a hard liver." Odus laughs. "Everything's all right with you, isn't it?" I don't answer. "You're not sick or anything?" Momentarily his voice is low, tender.

"No."

"So what are you saying?"

"Nothing. A joke."

"You always did have a morbid sense of humor." Again he's loud, aggressive.

"I don't know why I said that. Forget it."

"You ever make out a will?"

"Christ, Odus, talk about morbid. No."

"You should." From his point of view, why? If I die, if, for example, I'm fried in the electric chair, Odus, as my only living relative, will inherit everything.

When I was seven years old some men came up from Texas to do some exploratory drilling on our land. After six months of digging they found oil, and they eventually put up four pumps in what had formerly been our front yard. Unfortunately the wells outside our window didn't seem to be helping us out much financially. My father continued to fill prescriptions, six days a week, at the small pharmacy he owned, Lynch's Drugs, and my mother continued to tend the soda fountain and sandwich counter. We continued to live, as we always had, as "poor people." Daddy drove an old Ford pickup, because he couldn't afford a car, and our aging house hadn't been repaired in years—its once-yellow paint had long since faded, leaving behind ugly ocher streaks across the weathered boards. When Odus finished high school, Daddy couldn't afford to send him to college, so my brother worked pumping gas at night, and laying pipelines in the summer to pay his tuition at Central State College in Edmond, where he eventually received his degree in business administration.

It wasn't until he died of a heart attack at the age of sixty-two that we discovered my father had been a miser. My mother, who had always left the family finances completely to Daddy, who had never written a check in her life, and whose only experience with money management had been buying groceries from her meager weekly allowance, suddenly found herself to be a wealthy woman, certainly by Beldon standards. The oil wells, it turned out, had indeed been and continued to be extremely lucrative. In addition Daddy had secretly squirreled away two more small fortunes, one from the pharmacy profits, another from subsidies the government gave him not to farm his land.

Odus, by the time of Daddy's death newly married and armed with his degree in business administration, quickly took charge of my mother's finances. Mother did, however, learn to write checks, and she insisted on enjoying her newfound wealth. The first year after my father's death she bought, among other things, a double strand of pearls, a print by Raoul Dufy, and a burgundy and cream Lincoln Continental, and she donated a cherry tree to Beldon Park. The second year after his death she bought a condominium apartment on Lake Louise in Arkansas and announced her intention of spending the summer months there. When I finished high school Mother agreed, against Odus's objections, to pay for my expensive education at Yale, where I studied architecture with Charles Moore and Vincent Scully.

I returned to Oklahoma the summer I was twenty, between my junior and senior years at Yale, to work as an intern for the Tulsa Planning Commission. Susan came with me from New Haven, and we lived in a bungalow apartment near Peoria Street that Susan liked to refer to as "strictly Nathanael West." I returned to Oklahoma again when I was twenty-two after Odus called to say that Mother was dying of cancer. A week after I arrived she was gone. Michael Worth offered to fly out to be with me, but I said no, I'd be okay alone.

At Mother's funeral Odus and Judy, their kids Timmy and Cynthia, Aunt Em, and I sat in a special, screened enclosure as we listened to old Reverend Paul talk about my mother's courage and civic virtue, and a red-haired teenage girl sing "Abide with Me." Presumably this "family box" was designed to shield our grief from the other guests. After the services about half of those guests came out to the farm, where women from the Presbyterian Church served baked ham and potato salad and German chocolate cake from card tables set up in the living room. "Your mother looked just wonderful," one of the church women said as she patted me on the shoulder, "better than I'd seen her look in months." Toward the end of the reception Odus led me into our parents' bedroom where he and R. M. Tanner, a local lawyer, outlined the terms of my mother's will.

Mother more or less disinherited me. Perhaps angered by my less than attentive attitude during her final years (but who knew that she was dying?), and, I have no doubt, acting on the "advice" of my brother, Mother left almost everything to Odus, including the house and the farm and the burgundy and cream Lincoln Continental. I did receive a quarter share, along with Odus and Timmy and Cynthia, of the remaining oil dividends, but my dividends, and Timmy's and Cynthia's, were to be placed in an investment trust, controlled by Odus. I would immediately begin receiving a monthly check of three hundred dollars, Mr. Tanner explained, but the balance of my dividends, plus whatever profits Odus made (or lost?) investing that balance, I couldn't touch until I turned thirty-five. Mr. Tanner asked that day if I had any questions about the will. I said no. Sweat poured down the lawyer's forehead, and he looked nervously toward Odus, who was staring down at the faded, rose-patterned carpet. Mr. Tanner said that he wanted me to understand the reasoning behind the will, that my mother had felt that my brother should receive a "larger share" of her estate "in exchange" for the large amount of money she'd spent on me during the past six years. I looked toward my brother, but he continued staring at the floor, refusing to meet my gaze. My mother, Mr. Tanner continued, had felt that because I hadn't yet settled down . . . , but I interrupted Mr. Tanner and repeated that I had no questions about the will.

"Hey listen, don't smoke in here. The paint. You can go out in the hall."

"Sorry." I stub out the cigarette on the sole of my running shoe and return the butt to the pack.

"Sometimes I envy you."

"How so?"

"Seriously. What you've got is freedom. Like here you are, you can just take off and go wherever you please. Do what you want. You were always like that."

"I'm only here for a couple of days." My brother turns away from painting the pink wall to look down at me.

"I've got kids to feed, a business to run, alimony to pay . . ."

"A new house to keep up."

"A house to keep up. Damn straight."

"A mistress?"

"Damn straight. A mistress. Waitress down at Harding's okay? You think I'm some kind of winner or something? Believe it or not, if I had a choice, I'd trade places with you right now."

"Would you turn queer too?"

"I never put you down for that."

"No."

"I'm not interested in guys that way, but since you bring it up, it seems to me that you guys do okay. At least you don't get hassled so much for screwing around."

"Odus, you don't know a fucking thing about my life."

"Whose fault is that? From what I hear, you guys have a high old time."

Of course Odus isn't interested in guys "that way," but what to make of his obsession with "screwing around"? I wonder if women leave him for other reasons, if he uses "screwing around" as an excuse for others and for himself? A scene: I was having dinner one hot summer night in Tulsa, maybe six years ago, with Odus and Judy and some of their friends from Edmond. We were passing around a joint, and Odus was talking about the latest sport he'd taken up, boxing. He was enthusiastically describing the grammar of feinting and punching when Judy suddenly interrupted. "Well," she said, "it beats the hell out of pounding on me." Another scene: another hot summer night in Tulsa, the night Susan confessed that she'd slept with Odus. We yelled and screamed at each other for over an hour, a standard duet between betrayed and betrayer, between lovers on the outs. I taunted Susan. I asked her what my brother was like in bed, if he was really such a terrific fuck. Susan didn't answer immediately. I remember very clearly the huge, blue-tail fly she brushed away from her nose during the pause. "That's the strange part of it," she finally said, her voice low, breaking. "Yeah, he was terrific. He's so beautiful. But God, I hate him," and she burst into tears.

I shouldn't have told Odus I'd wait while he gets cleaned up. I don't want to have dinner with him at Harding's, and I don't want to meet his new lover, the waitress. Glancing around the alien, half-painted room, I suddenly realize how weary I am of remembering with my brother, of our old conflicts, the old clichés. I'm weary of Odus, of his new dream house, of his successes in business and his failures in love. Very deliberately I stick out my foot until it connects with an open half-gallon can of paint. Slowly I tip over the container and watch the oily mixture spread across the newspapers that Odus has haphazardly scattered about the floor. The paint runs through gaps onto the beige shag carpet, and I imagine it eventually seeping clear through the papers, leaving a terra-cotta imprint of yesterday's news across Odus's bedroom. I hear the splash of the shower and Odus singing, off-key, "Tonight's the Night," as I leave my brother's house.

ON JULY THIRD, after catching a matinee of *The Buddy Holly Story* at the Century Theater, I return to find that someone has searched my motel room. I make the discovery gradually, for the signs left by the intruder are not immediately apparent. I first notice the fiberglass drapes blowing in the wind. The sliding glass door behind them, which I distinctly remember closing before I left, is now partially open. In the bathroom a container of Percodans has been knocked over; in the closet the right pocket of my blue blazer has been turned out and my suitcase, although empty, has had its lock picked; and a Gideon Bible has been taken from a drawer and placed on top of the bedside table. As far as I can tell nothing has been taken from the room, including the fifteen hundred-dollar bills in the pocket of my black leather jacket and half an ounce of cocaine in an envelope at the bottom of my shaving kit. I pull back the sliding glass door completely and let the late afternoon breeze cool my cheeks. I look beyond the empty pool to the flat stretch of prairie and the sun, now setting, and the sky, now pink and gold and blood red.

YOU WONDER ABOUT the man, Mr. Jones, who built the house in 1929 and moved in just a few weeks before the market crashed. Was he mad, courageous, egomaniacal? Perhaps, like a lot of Frank Lloyd Wright's clients, Mr. Jones didn't quite know what he was getting into when he hired the master, who happened to be his cousin. Half a century later the enormous mass of glass and rose-tinted concrete blocks looms up against the night sky, bizarre, barbaric, and still unspeakably beautiful, a futuristic Mayan palace set down on the Oklahoma plains. Inside, moving through bare, shadowy spaces, are Mike and Lynda's guests, now visible through vertical strips of glass, now disappearing behind the carved concrete blocks. In the patio courtyard Mike's band, Empty Space, is playing from a makeshift stage, and kids are dancing in the bottom of the dilapidated, waterless pool. Marijuana fumes float through the hot, humid air.

It's odd to see Mike dressed in black leather pants and a leopard-print T-shirt, playing bass guitar. Empty Space is doing a number that's loud and heavy on percussion, "The Oil Industry in Crisis," written and sung by one Tom Tree. Tom is younger than Mike and me, maybe twenty or twenty-one. He's rather small, with ordinary, almost blunt facial features, and he's unflatteringly dressed in baggy pants and an old Hawaiian shirt. Yet he's a mesmerizing performer. He stalks the small stage like a caged animal, graceful and menacing. His tenor voice is almost too delicate for a rock singer, but there's nothing delicate about his passion or the lyrics of his song. It's an angry, disjointed tale about a man who's laid off from his job on an oil rig. The man takes out his frustration by beating his wife and kids. One day, unable to take any more abuse, the son attacks his father with a knife and blinds him. The song's refrain is the kid's speech before a judge:

> Send me away
> Send me away,
> Just forget what I did to dear old Dad,
> And forget what he did to me

and I can't listen to the band anymore, I feel as though I'm going to suffocate. Pushing my way through the crowd, I run into Lynda, who asks if I'm all right. She raises the sleeve of her caftan and wipes the sweat from my brow. I say that I just need something to drink, and Lynda points to a keg of beer sitting on a pedestal that Mr. Wright must have designed to hold a statue.

Empty Space is taking a break and Tom Tree and I are lying on our backs in the grass south of the house. Tom points out the constellations above us: Pegasus, Draco, Ursa Major, Virgo. Wonderful names. I ask Tom how he knows so much about the stars, and he says that he learned about them when he was a Boy Scout. I say that I was a Boy Scout too, but I don't remember learning about constellations, although I know how to tie lots of different knots. Tom laughs and confides that when he was twelve he was seduced by his scoutmaster.

"I guess that's fairly common, no? Not that it did me any harm. He just jerked off between my legs. Got me into his sleeping bag by saying that it would keep both of us warm. Actually I kind of liked the old guy."

I'm not sure why I start telling Tom about a little girl named Debbie, whom I read about in the newspaper a month or so ago. Debbie disappeared while she and her mother were shopping in a big department store in a San Jose mall. Her mother immediately notified the security guards, and they quickly sealed off the entire store. As the guards searched the premises, restless customers milled about, unable to leave, salespeople passed along gossip about the child and pointed out bargains, and nervous store officials tried to calm Debbie's mother, who was becoming more and more hysterical. After forty-five minutes a guard found a man, woman, and child in a seldom-used third-floor restroom near the furniture department.

Over the couple's vehement protests, the guard detained the three, and Debbie's mother was brought up to see if the little girl might be her missing daughter. The child was indeed Debbie, although the man and woman had already changed her clothes and cut off her long blond hair and sprayed it brown. They had also told the little girl that if she uttered a word, they'd kill her. The police came and took away Debbie's abductors and later announced that the two had been members of a "small-time" kidnapping and child pornography ring. Debbie, it was reported, uttered not a word for seven months.

"Makes you shiver. Maybe I won't move to California after all."

"It could have happened anywhere."

"In this country, I suppose so. People are too weird here. Maybe I'll go to Amsterdam. Of course, people are probably weird there too."

I ask a question, and Tom says that, yes, he wants to leave Empty Space, there are too many hassles with the others, too many conflicts. Mike and the rest are too interested in making a big deal album. And they've begun to reject some of his songs as too down, too political.

"It's like they forget about the music, you know? I just need to get away, experiment. On my own. Mike's a good guy, they all are, but they're getting weird. Too caught up."

Tom asks me what the punk scene is like in Los Angeles. I say that I live in San Francisco, not Los Angeles, and don't know much about the punk scene there. Tom asks if he might be able to stay with me if he comes to California, he doesn't know anyone there. "Just for a week or so, you know, until I can get things together." I say that would probably be all right. He asks if I'm listed in the phone book, and I say that I'm not, but I'll give him my number.

"Thanks. Maybe I'll come out in the fall." Someone has put on a tape of Paul Anka singing "Diana." Tom begins humming along, his high voice closer and louder than the music coming from the courtyard. I can also hear crickets chirping above the old song, and I can smell clean country smells, damp earth, freshly cut alfalfa, honeysuckle. I begin humming too. Then Tom and I start singing "Diana" together, our words sometimes preceding Paul Anka's, sometimes following his. Tom reaches out and places his hand in mine. Being alone in the dark out here with him and the music, looking up at the sky, momentarily erases the damages. There are tears in my eyes. Tom presses his palm more firmly into mine. I want him. Desire has been miraculously rekindled. But I'm still afraid. No, tonight is not possible.

A flare rises in the east and bursts into a pinwheel of light and color.

"Unbelievable," Tom says, "just like in the movies. Right on cue." I laugh uncontrollably and roll away from him, propelling my body through the grass, faster and faster until, breathless, I come to rest against a row of privet hedge. A second flare from the direction of the fairground fills the sky with a shower of red and white. Someone at the house has taken off the Paul Anka and put on a tape of Jimi Hendrix playing "The Star Spangled Banner." Tom Tree stands above me.

"Let's catch each other later," he says, "I've got to go shoot some crystal before we do our next set."

·—·—·— 33 ·—·—·—

I MUST HAVE fallen asleep. I see the moonlight streaming through the glass doors and then the body next to me. I think of Tom Tree before remembering that it's not Tom, of course, it's George, the traveling salesman. When I returned from Mike's party, drunk and stoned, I slipped into swimming trunks and jumped into the pool. Before I knew what was happening George was in the pool with me. Then suddenly we were in his room, on the bed where I am now, making love. I suppose that for weeks I'd thought of what it would be like to have sex again, had dreaded it, had feared that I'd be disgusted or hysterical or unable to function. But there I was clinging to George's big, strong body, whimpering like an animal, wanting him more than I'd ever wanted anyone. I remember a series of blows on my ass and George's tongue in my nostrils and both of us crying out obscenities. And I remember, afterward, being grateful to George. I did not, however, intend to fall asleep.

George lies face down, his big shoulders, almost flabby in repose, rising and falling with his breathing. A jagged scar runs from his right shoulder blade halfway down his back. Being careful not to wake him, I lift the sheet from my body and slip out of bed. On my feet, I realize that I'm still drunk. I move unsteadily about the room, searching in the half-light for my swimsuit. As I rifle through a pile of clothes on the dresser, a wallet, George's, falls from a pocket and its contents spill across the carpet. I glance toward the bed, but George is still sleeping peacefully, undisturbed. I gather up bills, plastic, slips of paper and try to stuff them back into the wallet, but they won't fit. I go into the bathroom, close the door behind me, and switch on the light, which is neon and bright and momentarily blinding. I see my blue Speedo hanging neatly on the handle of the shower door beside a pair of green trunks. I set George's wallet and its contents on the turquoise Formica sink counter and slip into my swimsuit.

I suspected, of course, that George gave me a false name. He did. A driver's license identifies the man sleeping in the next room as Richard F. Garr, 801 Sutter Street, San Francisco, California, 94113. Another card says that Richard Garr is licensed by the state of California as a private investigator. I look into the mirror above the sink and see a face that's frightened and angry and no longer drunk.

Flight
Two

34

IF YOU'VE KILLED once, I've heard, killing the second time comes easier. I suspect that this is not true. Maybe after the third time, or the fourth. In any case, I haven't yet entered the realm of multiple murder. I didn't want to kill Richard Garr, I just wanted to get away from him.

And so, in the still of the night, the desert stretches before me, an image of ultimate freedom, or emptiness. Only occasionally do I pass another car or, more often, a truck, and the only shapes on the horizon are huge boulders, black against the dove-gray sky. The endless white line down the middle of the highway becomes hallucinatory, a visual mantra. The voices on the radio become a mantra too, the metallic voices of insomniacs who phone in to complain about the president, to lament the passing of the drive-in movie, to champion laetrile and the Republic of South Korea, to accuse their spouses of adultery, their neighbors of sloth and stupidity and high treason.

"I know for a fact," a woman says, "that they've got a listening device in their basement. Directly connected to the Pentagon."

35

INTERIOR—HOSPITAL ROOM—DAY

CHERYL, in a hospital bed, still looking tired and weary. There are bouquets of flowers everywhere. CHERYL opens her eyes when she hears the door opening. JUDD enters, stands in front of the door. CHERYL looks away from him.

JUDD: *(moving toward CHERYL)* I'm so sorry. *(pause)* Cheryl?

JUDD sits down beside bed. Tears appear in CHERYL's eyes, but she still refuses to look at JUDD.

JUDD: Cheryl? Talk to me. Please.

CHERYL: Just go away.

JUDD: I just want to help you through this.

CHERYL: You want to help me through this? Now? Where were you when I needed you? When I needed you I was all alone.

JUDD: You know I didn't want it to be that way. I would have been here if I'd known. There was no way of knowing.

CHERYL: You should have been home with me where you belonged. You knew I needed you. But where were you? Out with Marilyn Keans in a nightclub.

JUDD: Who told you?

CHERYL: Does it matter?

JUDD: It's not what you think. Marilyn and I met in a *bar*. We needed to get some things straightened out.

CHERYL: I bet you did. *(begins crying)* I thought we were getting along better, I was really trying. But whenever Marilyn Keans calls, you still go running.

JUDD: It wasn't that way. I wanted to meet her—

CHERYL: That's supposed to console me? I'll never forgive you for this. Never.

JUDD: Cheryl, just listen to me. Let me tell you—

CHERYL: *(interrupting again)* I don't want to hear anything you have to say. You should have been here. Now I want you out of here.

JUDD: *(touching her shoulder)* Cheryl.

CHERYL: *(screaming and jerking away)* Get out of here. You're a monster. A monster. You'll pay for this.

JUDD: *(backing away)* All right. All right. Just remember the baby was mine too. *(now at door)* I'll be out here whenever you want to talk to me.

CHERYL: Get out!

CHERYL takes a vase of flowers from the bedside table and throws them. They crash against the door just as JUDD closes it, making his exit.

CHERYL: I'll make you pay for this Judd if it's the last thing I ever do.

CHERYL wipes tears from her face, picks up telephone, dials.

CHERYL: *(into phone)* Hello. Marilyn? *(pause)* That doesn't really matter now, does it? I want to see you right away. Be here at the hospital in thirty minutes. *(pause)* Just skip the condolences Marilyn. I want to see you. *(pause)* I don't care. Just be here. In thirty minutes.

CHERYL slams down the receiver.

"You want to run through it again?" I ask.

"No," Karina says, "I think I've got it down. Not that it matters anyway. They don't care if you use the exact words. I can always fake it." She rises from the sofa, tosses the script down, and goes into the kitchen. I hear her opening and closing the refrigerator door.

"You have any plans for today?" she calls above the whir of the electric blender.

"You have any plans for today?" Karina repeats when she returns to the living room. She stares down at me, the expression in her violet eyes unreadable.

"No plans," I finally answer.

Karina drinks some of the foamy liquid she mixes every morning.

"Cal, it's just that I don't exactly understand what it is you *do* all day long."

I look out the big leaded window to the Spanish courtyard where the gray and yellow tom is playing at the fountain. Perched on its rim, the cat leans down and swats at something in the water, arches back and shakes out his wet paw, then leans down and swats again.

"Think about coming with me to Ricky's on Sunday," Karina says.

36

WHAT I DO all day long is this: I listen to music, most often Bach, I smoke cigarettes, and I wait for the arrival of Mr. Richard F. Garr, licensed private investigator. Every day at two P.M. I walk down the hill to the Las Palmas newsstand on Hollywood Boulevard to buy the San Francisco papers, then, back in Karina's apartment, I search through columns of print for new information, for stories about what I have come to think of as "the case." As yet the papers have provided no new information; there are no stories.

· — · — · — 37 · — · — · — ·

HOLLYWOOD'S OLDEST-ESTABLISHED restaurant is deserted in an off hour, three in the afternoon, and the adjoining cocktail lounge has only three customers. Two silver-haired gentlemen sit at one end of the long mahogany bar, I sit at the opposite end, and between us stands the bartender, also silver-haired and dressed in a black tie and dinner jacket. I signal him to bring me my fourth Jack Daniel's on the rocks. I'm reluctant to leave the cool darkness and the preserved-in-amber elegance of Musso and Frank's for the ready-to-riot crowd, the din, the brain-boiling heat of Hollywood Boulevard, and for the sweltering boredom of Karina's non-air-conditioned apartment. This morning the radio announced a second-stage smog alert and predicted that the temperature would hit 104, which I'm sure it has. Karina suggested that I spend the day at the beach, and I said maybe I would. In fact, traveling more than a few blocks, getting into my car and actually *going* somewhere seems to me more and more impossible. Although perhaps coming into Musso and Frank's is a start. A step, as Dr. Redman would have said, in the right direction. As Dr. Redman would say.

I can hear the voices but not the words of the men at the end of the bar, and I can hear, as the bartender hands me my drink, the high-pitched laughter of the taller of the two. The men are formally and, for any place on the Boulevard except this restaurant, incongruously dressed: dark suits, conservative ties, starched white shirts. Both have the too-well-preserved looks and the theatrical air common to aging actors and old-time queens. A newspaper sits on the bar beside them, probably a trade paper, and I imagine their conversation turning on the decline and fall of the "industry."

The maitre d' ushers a fourth customer into the cocktail lounge. The newcomer is tall, thin, fortyish, and has sandy, rather unkempt hair. As his watery blue eyes rest on the silver-haired gentlemen and then, more lingeringly, on me, he takes a handkerchief from the pocket of his khaki pants and wipes sweat from his forehead. I turn away from his gaze and light a cigarette. When a waiter appears from the restaurant I look around to see that he's taking the order of the newcomer, who's settled into one of the big booths directly behind me.

I wonder if the two gentlemen at the end of the bar have been coming to Musso and Frank's since its heyday in the thirties. Maybe they were in the movies then, maybe they were even "names" once and have gold stars on the sidewalk outside to prove it. Of course, it's just as likely that the men are insurance salesmen who've knocked off early to celebrate landing a client, or that they're dentists visiting from

Pittsburgh or hog farmers from Dubuque. Even if the two are actors, it's quite possible that they're still working, they certainly look prosperous enough. Still, I prefer the romantic drama of has-beens meeting daily at the bar to discuss the action of which they're no longer a part, to remember their glory days.

Odd the versions of people you prefer to file, however sentimental, the images of them you find yourself creating, however ignorant. As another example, this: When I think of the man I killed, when he comes smashing back into my brain, I no longer see him lying on the floor of his nightmare Maybeck house. No, I see him sitting at an old metal desk in a concrete-floored warehouse, the kind of place in which I imagine a shipping clerk works. Surrounded by ceiling-high stacks of cardboard boxes, wearing a shirt that exposes the alabaster flesh of his neck and arms, the fat man bends over stacks of paper, fills out forms in triplicate.

Only after I turn left on Cherokee and start up the hill do I realize that I'm being followed. I could feel the sandy-haired man's eyes on my back in the bar, and he must have come out right after me, then faded into the tourists and assorted rough trade on the Boulevard. When a car backfires and I glance back, I see him walking past Love's, just half a block behind me. After the man sees that I've spotted him he makes no attempt to disappear. On the contrary. He looks straight at me, even smiles, I think, and seems to increase his speed as he moves away from the crowd and comes toward me. Now would be the time to run, but run where? And what would be the point? I look to the palm-lined street at the top of the hill and keep walking. Absurdly, I remember the words of the Twenty-third Psalm, and I remember Aunt Em's voice.

By the time I reach Yucca the man's right behind me, I can hear his labored progress, I can feel or at least I imagine that I can feel his breath on the back of my neck.

"Gotcha!" he says as he pulls up beside me and thrusts his face into mine. I stop. I look into his watery eyes and wait for him to speak again. But when he does, I can't understand what he's saying. His words are an incomprehensible babble. It's as though he's speaking in tongues, or in pig latin. Then just as suddenly as his babbling began, it stops. The man laughs, a single, high-pitched cackle.

"Gotcha!" he says again. "What you up to?" It's at this point that I begin to realize the man's not, as I thought, a cop or another private detective from San Francisco. I try to walk away from him, but he follows me, keeps pace.

"What do you want?" The man leers. "I'm not interested in being picked up."

"You think that's what I'm trying to do? Trying to pick you up?"

"That's what I think."

"Think again."

"Why'd you follow me from the bar?"

"I followed you, did I? Not me."

"Good. So why don't you get lost now?" The man starts babbling, speaking in tongues again. I try to ignore him.

"You know what your problem is?" He's in normal voice now. "You're insecure. I've met lots of boys like you. Insecure."

"I don't need someone like you to tell me what my problems are." I'm shaking with anger.

"Hit a nerve, huh?"

"Fuck off."

"I used to eat ones like you for breakfast, pretty boy."

"Just get the fuck away from me."

"Free country. I've got just as much right to walk down this sidewalk as you, wouldn't you say? Wouldn't you say that's true?" I clench my right hand into a fist and slam it into his face hard. His head jerks sideways and a big red patch appears above his jawline.

"Fuckin' A," someone shouts. I turn and see that we're standing in front of a rundown bungalow apartment building. Three black kids, one boy, two girls, are watching us from a weed-strewn patch of lawn.

"Yeah man, hit him again," says the boy. I land another blow in the man's freckled face. It catches him just below his left eye, and he staggers backward, trips, and falls to the sidewalk. The kids shout with delight. The man lunges at my legs, tries to pull me to the ground. I jump free, then land a kick in his ribs, another in his face. Blood pours from his nose.

"You've made me bleed," he says with surprise. He pulls a white handkerchief from his khaki pants, dabs at his face. "You kicked me. You made me bleed."

"Good. Now get up and get away from me you stupid fuck before I tear you apart." The man stretches the now bloody handkerchief across his face like a veil and remains on the ground. "I said get up." He slowly rises to his feet, staggers, looks at me with a combination of fear and insolence. He begins speaking in tongues again, but this time more quietly, more to himself than to me.

"Shut up. I said shut up." The man quits babbling. "Now get the hell away from me. Walk! Walk!" I'm yelling at the top of my lungs. The kids are squealing. A woman appears in a doorway behind a broken screen.

"You all stay out of this," she shouts.

"Shit," says one of the girls, "just faggots cutting each other."

I follow the sandy-haired man as he makes his way unsteadily up the hill. Periodically he glances back to see if I'm still behind him, then makes flapping motions with his arms, like a bird, waving the now-red handkerchief behind him. I trail him all the way to Franklin, enjoying the man's suffering, his fear.

38

WHEN THE BEDROOM door opens a shaft of light shines on the heavy oak beams twenty feet above me and filters down to the sofa where I lie uncovered in the heat. I hear footsteps move across the balcony's wood floor, and I look up to see a naked man cautiously descending the open staircase. Downstairs he knocks against a parsons table holding a lamp as he moves to the tape deck beside the fireplace. He squats and fumbles noisily through a stack of cassettes on the floor. When he glances toward me, I close my eyes. I hear more fumbling, then see pink light against the backs of my eyelids.

"Sorry," a low voice says. I open my eyes to an illuminated room and to a man with a tapered swimmer's body. Thick dark hair covers his chest, abdomen, legs, he's too furry for my tastes. "Just changing the tape, buddy. Couldn't see. Sorry." He grins sheepishly, he's probably drunk or coked out. I pull the sheet up to my waist and close my eyes again. I'd prefer that Karina not bring people here, but, of course, I can't say anything, it's her apartment. Better, I suppose, to have to listen to Karina and a trick fucking than to have to make conversation with her and her "unit publicist" over drinks, as I did last Saturday night. Maybe I should move to the YMCA. When whatever-his-name-is finally snaps a cassette into the machine, the beginning of a Rolling Stones song drifts down from the bedroom speakers. The light goes off, and I hear him go back up the stairs, cross the balcony, close the bedroom door.

Every night I lie awake on the sofa here, and sometimes I think about the nights I lay awake on the sofa after I found out that Susan and Odus were lovers. I believe I thought then that I was punishing Susan by refusing to sleep with her. It's true that she cried herself to sleep every night, but in retrospect I suspect that her tears were not perhaps solely, or even mainly, a result of my refusal to come to her bed. In any case, Susan left after a week, went back to spend the rest of the summer with her family in Darien, Connecticut, cutting short her stay in Tulsa by two months.

I can hear them thrashing about above me, and I can make out, just barely,

> *I bet your mama was*
> *A tent show queen*
> *And all her girlfriends*
> *Were sweet sixteen*
> *I'm no schoolboy*
> *But I know what I like*
> *You should have heard me*
> *Just around midnight.*
> *Brown sugar . . .*

From outside come the muffled sounds of Saturday-night traffic on Franklin, the whir of motors, the slap of rubber against concrete, the honking of horns, the squeal of brakes—sex music of another sort. I throw off the sheet, touch my jockey shorts. Nothing. I take my hand away and stare up at the beamed ceiling of the apartment where one of the Talmadge sisters once lived, the apartment where a scene of a Rudolph Valentino movie was once shot.

CHEZ LENA READS a small brass plaque beside the entrance gate. We step into a sun-dappled courtyard where fuchsia and bougainvillea and a lemon tree grow and beyond that, through open French doors, into a large white living room that overlooks the Pacific. About three dozen people are gathered here and on an adjoining deck. Several of the men look like they model for *Gentlemen's Quarterly,* and, according to Karina, they probably do, and a few of the younger women are as striking as the one I'm escorting. In contrast to Karina, however, who's slight, ivory-skinned, brunette, these are beauties in the Southern California mode: long-legged, golden-tressed, tanned. Although the women's tans mean, again according to Karina, that they're probably not getting much work. "If they ever get any. Work that is. Lot of people out here *pretending* to be actresses." Karina is not in a particularly charitable mood. As we make our way to the bar set up between the living and dining rooms, I notice a few more decorative guests. A thin young woman who wears a wet suit and has platinum hair that's streaked with blue and pink is standing beneath a fishtail palm with an equally thin young man, bare-chested, who has studded wrist bands and a mohawk haircut; and, sitting alone in front of a fireplace on a white canvas sofa that sets off her gleaming black skin, is a woman who looks like Grace Jones and for all I know may *be* Grace Jones.

As a waiter who could also be a *GQ* model makes our drinks, Perrier with lime for Karina, a double bourbon for me, we're approached by a short, balding man wearing Bermuda shorts and a USC T-shirt. He and Karina kiss before she introduces him as Ricky Blumenthal, the producer of the new *Rise and Fall of Legs Diamond.*

"Actually," Ricky says, as he grasps me in an old-fashioned hippie handshake, "we're thinking now of calling it *Rise and Fall.* You know? Short. Classic. Or maybe just *Diamond.* Good, here are your drinks." Ricky wants to know if Karina minds coming back to the library with him to meet a potential backer, and without waiting for an answer, he steers her away from the bar.

"Microchips," I hear Ricky say as I watch his squat retreating backside. Karina looks over her shoulder and gestures with a combination wave and shrug. I move to the only noncrowded area of the room, the space in front of the fireplace, and sit down on the white sofa beside the woman who looks like Grace Jones. She studies me with enormous dark eyes, then extends her hand. Her long nails are lacquered black, a shade that's almost an exact match for her skin.

"Lilibeth Hughes." Her throaty voice has an "upper-class" stage accent.

"Cal Lynch."

"Are you an actor, Cal?" I tell Lilibeth yes, I am an actor. She wants to know who my agent is, and I say Jim Schuman, the man who represented me when I was doing theater in New York. Lilibeth nods, as though she recognizes his name, and tells me who *her* agent is in a tone that makes clear I should recognize his name too. I nod.

"I've heard he's good." Lilibeth, pleased with my response, smiles, revealing dazzlingly white teeth, pink gums.

"He *is* good. In only six months since I've been with Eric—I've only been in town for six months, you understand—he's already sent me up for four major commercials. I'm sure I'll get one eventually." In her enthusiasm a faint Southern lilt creeps through the stagey accent. I ask Lilibeth where she lived before she came to Los Angeles. Instead of answering she looks toward the ocean and smiles in a way that I think is meant to be mysterious. Suddenly she leans against my shoulder and whispers conspiratorially in my ear.

"Isn't this place just paradise? Just between you and me, Calvin, I've never been in a house in Malibu before that had a double lot."

"Caleb," I whisper into her ear, "and I've never

been in a house in Malibu before." Lilibeth jerks away from me, frowns indignantly, as though I've made a particularly obscene proposition.

"Please excuse me," she says coldly, "while I go mingle." As Lilibeth strides elegantly away, I look across the room to see two tanned, middle-aged women watching me with bemusement. I grin at them, shrug. Their guess is as good as mine.

A tall thin man comes up and asks, demands to know really, where Karina is. I glare at him. He explains that he's Larry Kaplan, Karina's agent, and that he saw us come in together.

"I know who you are, Cal. Karina's talked about you. Told me you're looking for an agent. Interesting look. We should have lunch." I start to say that I'm not looking for an agent and don't want to have lunch, but Larry interrupts and again demands to know where Karina is. I tell him that she and Ricky Blumenthal are with someone into microchips. Larry's skin stretches tightly across his high cheekbones.

"Goddamn that Blumenthal. Karina shouldn't have to be talking to money. What the fuck's Blumenthal think he's doing anyway? Trotting her out like some goddamn whore? And *I* should be in on that meeting, I'd better find them. But listen, Cal, I'm serious. Send me your portfolio and some tape and we'll talk. A word to the wise: That mean, hard look is interesting but don't overdo it."

The young congressman leans on a silver-tipped cane, "a replica of one that FDR had." The congressman has beautiful, unlined skin, curly hair that's prematurely gray, and the upper torso of a body builder. He asks if I'd like to go into the bathroom with him. I say I think not.

"Whatever you want. I saw you when you first arrived with that new actress. What's her name?"

"Karina Brown."

"Right. Beautiful woman. I hear she's going to be in this new picture Ricky and George are planning. *The Rise and Fall* or *Diamond* or whatever it's called. I hope it works out for them, big backers of mine you know. Although I hear the financing's still shaky."

"I wouldn't know."

"Are you an actor then?"

"No."

"What do you do?"

"I'm in business."

"Yes?"

"Oil. Real estate. Condominium developments."

"That's spectacular. If Karina Brown doesn't make it, it's nice to know she has someone to fall back on. Risky business our friends are in. Are you sure you wouldn't like to come with me to the bathroom? No strings attached."

"I don't think so. Thanks."

A few bronzed bodies still lie on towels, soaking up the last rays of the sun, and two small boys race along the sand, a Japanese kite trailing behind them. Each of the kite's cellophane, tail-like sections is a different primary color, red and green and blue and yellow, and as I watch these twisting in the wind I see a living creature against the sky, a huge exotic fish slithering through incredibly pure water in a world turned upside down.

Beyond the sunbathers and the boys and the row of houses on stilts, the land curves to form a reef that extends into the ocean. I set my half-empty glass of bourbon on the ground and climb over slippery rocks to find myself on another, narrower strip of beach. Here the face of a cliff, gold and silver in the light, rises straight up from the sand, and the area is deserted except for a woman sitting on top of a big rock near the tideline, gazing out to sea. I don't want to disturb the woman, but she turns around, as though sensing my presence, and when she sees me, waves. I approach, and when the woman looks down and asks if I'm enjoying the party, I recognize her as one of the guests I saw earlier.

"Just out for a walk," I tell her.

"Me too. Want to come up?" she asks with a pronounced Southern accent. She extends her hand and helps me to the top of the rock. I settle myself on the ledge beside her. The woman's probably in her late thirties, although she's well, and no doubt expensively, preserved. Her narrow face, tanned and freckled and lineless, is devoid of makeup except for a hint of pink on slightly too thin lips. Large dark glasses obscure her eyes. The two of us sit in silence watching the roll of the waves, the glassy moving planes of the ocean. Her fingers play idly with a thin, gold chain on her left ankle.

"I saw you talking to that tall black girl," she says after a few minutes.

"I know you did." Then the woman laughs, a rich, honeyed sound.

"What was it you said to her?"

"That's just it. I don't know. Only that I'd never

been to Malibu before." I shrug and we both laugh, and laugh some more, and for some reason we're soon almost hysterical.

"No, we have to stop," she gasps and places her hand on my arm. "We shouldn't be making fun of her."

"Are we? And why not? Lilibeth," I shout, "her name's Lilibeth." Eventually our hysterical laughter subsides.

"I'm just an old-fashioned, still-guilty liberal," the woman says after she catches her breath.

"What?"

"It's just that I grew up in the South, as you may have gathered, and sometimes I can't help remembering . . ."

"Remembering?"

"Oh, never mind. I'm slightly drunk."

"No, so am I. Go on."

"Well, Lilibeth's pretentious, but who among us is not? And I know for a fact that she came to town not very long ago from some teachers college in Louisiana, and when I see someone like her I can't help looking back, remembering what it used to be like in the South.

"I remember watching television one day, for example—I was young then, a teenager, I guess— during the big trouble over integration in Little Rock. An angry mob of whites was trying to prevent the black kids from getting into the school, and the scene was bloody and awful. And I watched this on TV in a room full of my relatives, all of whom were laughing."

"And you were the sensitive one?"

"Oh no, I wasn't sensitive at all. I was laughing too.

170

I quit laughing soon, of course, everything changed for me, but still . . ."

"But I don't see how that relates to Lilibeth. She could have the heart of a viper. Probably does from what I saw."

"Oh, I know she does."

"So you grew up in Little Rock?"

"No, Jackson, Mississippi."

"Well, I think I understand. I'm from Oklahoma." She studies my face.

"So we've both traveled quite a distance, haven't we? What's your name, Okie?"

"Cal."

"I'm Lena."

"As in Chez Lena?" She laughs her rich, full laugh again.

"Don't blame me for that! My illiterate ex-husband put that silly sign up."

"So how come you skipped out on your own party, Lena?"

"Oh, I'm not doing a Leslie Gore or anything. It's not really *my* party. Ricky Blumenthal . . ."

"I met Ricky."

"Ricky works for George, my ex-husband, actually we're still married, but separated—Ricky wanted to have the party here to impress some backers for this new film they're trying to get off the ground. Since George's production company actually owns the house I didn't really think I should tell Ricky no. As long as the caterers clean up, it's a small price to pay. George has been very generous to me." Lena laughs.

As the evening tide rolls in and the sky and the hills to the west turn gauzy pink, I learn that George is in

London now, working on another film, and that he and Lena have been separated for three years. I learn that their fifteen-year-old daughter Georgina is the girl with the blue-and-pink hair, and that the kid with the mohawk haircut is Georgina's twenty-one-year-old boyfriend, of whom Lena disapproves. I learn that Lena and Georgina spend most of the year in an apartment on Central Park West in Manhattan and only come out here in the summer. I learn that Lena, trained as a musicologist and as an organist, occasionally gives recitals in New York, and that this summer she's filling in at Sunday masses at a Catholic church in Rancho Park while the congregation's regular organist recovers from a suicide attempt he made while on a bad acid trip. And Lena learns a few things about me.

"We'd better get down," she says, "before we're completely surrounded and carried all the way to China." I jump into swirling, calf-high water and reach up for Lena. As she gets off the rock I pull her to me, run my palm along her white sweater, grazing full breasts. Lena leans against my shoulder as we make our way back up the beach.

"I like you," Lena says at the bottom of the steps to her house.

"I like you too."

"If you want to spend some time at the beach while you're in town, you're welcome to stay here." Lena removes her glasses, but I'm facing the setting sun and can't make out her expression or tell the color of her eyes. "There are," she adds, "several extra bedrooms."

* * *

"Goddamn you," Karina says as she navigates furiously through heavy traffic on the Santa Monica Freeway. "I really thought you'd gone out and drowned yourself. Finally done it."

"I told you, I just took a walk on the beach. What makes you think I'm suicidal?"

"What makes me think you're suicidal? Every night I come home from work and you're drunk and stoned on God knows what. You leave pills scattered about everywhere, a little trail of destruction. You won't talk, you hardly eat, and really, every time I open the door at night, I'm afraid I'm going to find you dead, OD'd."

"I was walking on the beach. Okay? Waiting for your meeting to end."

"I thought you were with Lena James."

"Yes, I was talking to her."

"For two hours? You stay with me for two weeks, maybe talk to me for a total, a *total* of fifteen minutes during that time. Then suddenly you come out of your catatonia and talk for *two hours* to a woman you've never met before? And what were you telling everyone? About being an oilman or something? Ricky asked me to talk to you about investing in *Rise and Fall,* for Christ's sake."

"Well, I hear the financing's still shaky." Karina slams on the brakes, ostensibly to avoid plowing into a yellow mini-bus that crosses into our lane.

"Cal, I don't know what to do for you anymore. You're driving me crazy."

"I didn't know it was that bad."

"Just let me know what's wrong."

"Nothing's wrong."

173

THE BEARDED MAN sitting behind the front counter in the bile-colored room chain-smokes unfiltered Camels and watches in a convex detective mirror as I, his only customer, move slowly down the long, narrow aisles, studying the racks of magazines. Light from old-fashioned neon tubes hanging from the ceiling throws the photographs of bodies and of body parts into garish, almost hallucinatory relief. A lot of the magazines have alliterative titles such as *Backroom Blonds, Sexy Strangers, Hardhat Heaven,* and many of them have "themes" connected to presumably macho professions and pursuits, the above-mentioned *Hardhat Heaven,* for example, and also *Roundup at the K-Y Corral* and *Surf's Up* and *Cops and Robbers.* Other titles bluntly cater to specific fetishes, fantasies: *Black Men, Eleven Inches, Young Ass, Piss Party.* There are photographs of tanned young bodies frolicking in rivers and mountains, and there are photographs of pale bodies in black leather torturing one another in urban caves. In short, there's a whole inventory of male-on-male desires here, a repertoire of images from which to choose. My own desire that afternoon is a specific one, although not, I suppose, a simple desire, nor one that can necessarily be fulfilled. I want to see a photograph of Buddy.

As I scan the covers of the magazines and flip through the pages of a few of the more promising ones, I recognize certain faces, bodies. For most of these I have only the recognition itself, not specific memories, they're men I've seen in bars, perhaps, or in gyms, or on the street, or in other magazines, and maybe one or two of them are men I tricked with once and then forgot. A few faces I connect with times, places, names. I see a bartender who used to give me free drinks at the Eagle in New York, now shorn of his beard and his clothes and transported to a beach in Maui, and I see David, from the gym in San Francisco, now up in a sling being fisted by a redhead, whose beautiful freckled face is also vaguely familiar. And, inevitably, there's a copy of *Cycle Cops,* a magazine composed of stills from one of the movies Max made. "Christ," Max said the day the "complimentary" copy arrived from the producer, "they didn't tell us they were going to turn the goddamn thing into a book too! I ought to hit the bastards up for more money." On the cover Max, wearing a California highway patrolman's uniform, straddles a Harley Davidson as he's blown by a young guy with shaggy brown hair and a mole like Robert De Niro's. A helmet and mirrored sunglasses partially obscure Max's face, and there's a black circle over the spot where his cock meets the kid's mouth.

However, I'm not here to linger over faces from *that* past. It's the more recent past I'm seeking, and, after thirty minutes of careful and systematic looking, my hunch about Buddy surprisingly pays off—I find the photograph I want. Actually there's a series of photographs of him in a magazine called *Rock Hard.* Buddy: also known as Raymond Bell, here called "Jerry," the boy the Berkeley police are seeking—or perhaps are now holding on suspicion—in connection with the shooting of Marcus J. Irving. Buddy, the physical facts as further revealed in these photographs: a mass of curly blond hair framing a round face that still has lingering traces of baby fat; small, deep-set brown eyes fringed with pale, almost invisible lashes; thick pink lips; of short stature, at least compared with the other men in the photographs; a hairless, undeveloped chest, chunky, undefined legs, but muscled back, shoulders, and arms that look like they were developed from sports or from labor rather than from weights; an uncircumcised cock that's thick but shorter-than-average both flaccid and erect; a big, rounded ass that's featured—with cheeks spread—in many of the photographs; and hands and feet that seem unusually large for someone of Buddy's size.

Rock Hard tells a story in pictures about a long-maned rock singer who picks up a young hitchhiker (Buddy). As the two of them make it, in a variety of ways, in the back seat and on the hood of the singer's big black Lincoln, the limo's uniformed driver watches impassively. Later, in a cheap motel room the driver finally gets out of his uniform and joins Buddy and the singer in bed. Then, on the road again, the three are stopped by a highway patrolman (that recurring icon), who leads them to what looks like an abandoned barn where all four men make hay, so to speak, then change partners, and make some more hay, and change partners again, et cetera. In most of these photographs Buddy reveals only two facial expressions, a blatant, almost campy leer, and a strange, faraway look that could indicate either sexual abandon or boredom. In one photograph, however, he shows another face. It's a picture toward the beginning of the magazine and the only one in which Buddy's shown alone. At this point in the narrative Buddy still has on jeans and a T-shirt, and he stands on the side of a highway in front of a tree-shaded rest stop. One of his big hands holds a backpack, the other is curled in the standard thumb-up gesture of hitching. Sunlight catches highlights in the golden hair and plays on a face that is, for once, relaxed. Buddy smiles and seems to be pleading, but pleading gently, with someone just off camera.

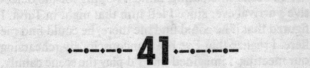

THE RING AT the door that I've been expecting comes at 4:10 on the afternoon of July twenty-third. It's a buzz, actually, from the front gate. I freeze and flash immediately on the handsome, weatherbeaten face of

Richard Garr. Of course, it's more probable that the person buzzing is a polltaker or a Jehovah's Witness or a mailman with a postage due letter, but somehow I know, I can feel in my bones that the man out there's the duplicitous detective from San Francisco who followed me to Tulsa and has caught up with me again here. I put out a cigarette, wave my arms against the snaky lines of smoke caught in the shafts of light escaping through closed Venetian blinds, and I lift the needle from the third side of *The Art of the Fugue*. My hand shakes badly, metal scrapes against plastic, and an electronic whine echoes in the stillness between the third and fourth buzzes. There's a fifth buzz, longer, more insistent than the others. Then there's silence.

I exhale loudly, suddenly aware that I've been holding my breath. Weakly I sink back into the sofa, and as the silence holds and my head clears, I try to calm my bogeyman fears. It's not at all likely that the person buzzing was Richard Garr.

I've been anticipating, almost hoping for the detective's arrival ever since I left him that night in Tulsa. I figured that if he could find me there, he could find me here. I realize that I've been unconsciously rehearsing our meeting. I imagined that I'd play the scene calmly, that I'd face the inevitable with grace, that I'd surrender instead of run this time, give up with a sigh of relief. That's what I imagined; but when I thought the detective was waiting for me at the gate I wasn't ready to give up at all. No, I was scared, and I was prepared to do whatever I needed to do to remain free. Am prepared.

So perhaps I should take off again, leave here before the detective or someone else really does trace me to Karina. I could drive up the coast, find a quiet little beach town, I've heard that Santa Cruz is nice. I'd hide out there for awhile, then, after bypassing San Francisco, drive through Washington and Oregon to Vancouver. Maybe from Canada I should fly to Europe, to Paris perhaps, or Amsterdam. Or maybe I'll go to Africa. I picked up a Frenchman in a bar in New York once who was a philosophical anarchist and a professional thief and a wanderer. He described traveling across the Sahara, the lulling and weightless feeling you get from the endless, unchanging miles of sky and sand. He said that you lose all sense of space and time there, that weeks pass, or maybe months, you're not sure which and don't care as your ego dissolves into the landscape.

Of course, there's a problem: money. I withdrew most of the money from my savings account before I left San Francisco and there's not a lot of that left, and I'm beginning to reach the limit on all of my charge cards. I can't sell the Honda unless I return to San Francisco, since payments are still due, or unless I find some con man, who wouldn't give me a fair price. Perhaps I could pick up some kind of work in Vancouver, although . . .

I hear footsteps against the hollow tiles of the courtyard. They're coming toward me. I cross the room on tiptoe and flatten myself against the front door. The footsteps, unhurried, inexorable, come closer and closer. A shadow moves against the Venetian blinds of the big front window, then the footsteps stop on the other side of the door. Only two inches of carved oak separate me from the bogeyman. I wait for a knock, but none comes. Glancing down I see, with horror and despair, that the iron bolt is turned upwards, which means that the door's unlocked. How could I be so goddamn stupid! Slowly I reach out and touch the lock, fearful that he'll hear the movement of limb through air, the impact of flesh against iron. I close my moist thumb and index finger around the lock. If I turn it now, he'll hear and know for certain that I'm inside, so I stand poised, waiting for him to make the first move. I stare at the doorhandle, alert for the slightest sign. If he tries to open the door, I hope that I can jam the lock into place before he pushes through. But there's no movement and no sound from the man on the other side.

More silence. And more. Then he moves. His shadow passes the window again, he walks back across the courtyard toward the gate. I wipe away the sweat running into my eyes. I want to look out at my unwanted visitor's retreating back, but I'm afraid he'll glance back and see me if I crack the blinds.

·—·—·—· **42** ·—·—·—·

THE SEA BREEZE is faintly tinged with the acrid scent of kelp and waves pound rhythmically against the shore as I close my eyes and allow my mind to drift, empty out, come to rest. Then—later?—she pulls a soft quilt across my shoulders and whispers my name. I turn to see her narrow face above me, brow raised quizzically over green eyes, thin lips parted in a half smile. Pulling amber-colored hair away from her face, she bends and places her mouth against mine, then pulls away. Behind her the pale, softly lit room is reflected in a wall of glass that seems to shimmer against the blackness of the ocean and the sky.

"I'll see you in the morning," Lena says.

"Aren't you sleeping here?" As she shakes her head no, the amber-colored hair falls to her shoulders, brushes her cheeks. She starts to rise from the bed, but I reach out and encircle her waist.

"Stay. Just a little longer." She looks at me, then turns away her head. I run my fingers down her tanned back, tracing her spine. "Please." Lena sinks back onto the bed. She props herself against the padded headboard and pulls the pale blue quilt up to her neck.

"Cold?" From a travertine table beside the bed Lena takes a cigarette, lights it, exhales, passes it to me.

"I'm afraid we may have jumped the gun tonight," she says.

"Are you kidding? I think we've shown remarkable self-restraint." Lena shakes her head, frowns. She's not kidding.

I surprised Lena and surprised myself by appearing at her door last Thursday evening. I left Karina's under cover of darkness that night, drove up into the Hollywood Hills, and made a number of quick turns through the labyrinth of streets to lose anyone who might be following me. Streetlamps were sparse up there and irregularly placed, but through heavy foliage I could glimpse tungsten lamps illuminating carports, and, behind various-sized panes of glass, I could see the glow of, perhaps, domestic tranquility. At the end of one cul-de-sac, beyond a row of conifers, the entire city of angels stretched out below me, a vast carpet of light enveloping the earth in a gridlike pattern as far as the eye could see. Then I found my way back to Sunset and drove west and down all the way to the Coast Highway. I planned to travel all night, but I hit a bank of fog just beyond Santa Monica and on impulse took the Malibu Beach Road turnoff and found Lena's house. I don't know what I expected, I suppose I didn't really expect much of anything, didn't even know if Lena would remember her carelessly-proffered invitation of the week before. Her initial reaction to my unannounced visit was indeed cool and understandably wary, but she politely offered me a drink, and after we talked over a couple of more drinks and she found out that I planned to drive through the fog at least as far as Santa Barbara, Lena insisted that I spend the night. The next morning over breakfast she said that I was welcome to stay for a few more days if I wanted. I've been here ever since.

Lena and I have developed, by unspoken agreement, a sort of daily ritual, or perhaps it's more accurate to say that I've developed a ritual that fits into her existing one, I don't know. In any case, we tend to avoid each other during the mornings and afternoons: I lie in the sun and swim, and I brood and try not to brood; Lena seems to spend her days running errands and reading and cooking and arguing with her teenage daughter and, mainly, practicing at the electric organ in the library. We don't really get together until around eight in the evening. The daughter always seems to eat early or to eat out, so it's only Lena and I who sit down to the elegant little suppers she prepares, poached salmon last Friday, tarragon-flavored chicken on Saturday, shrimp Creole on Sunday, veal sirloin on Monday, sweetbreads with artichoke hearts tonight. We sit at the glass-topped table overlooking the ocean until two or three in the morning, lingering over our food, watching the candles flame, then gutter out, talking, talking endlessly, polishing off two bottles of wine every night, which is a bottle each. Hovering over these tense and drunken and wonderful evenings has been of course the present-from-the-beginning question: Should we or should we not sleep together? I think that the food and the drinking and the increasingly intimate and urgent conversation has been our means of both searching for and postponing—postponing for whatever reasons of fear and delicacy I'm not certain—the answer to that question. Tonight, however, something broke, the uncertainty ended—or so I thought. When we rose from the table around three we finally embraced, then lay against each other on the cold tile floor of the dining room for a long while, then moved to "my" bedroom, undressed each other, and had sex. But now Lena's telling me that she thinks we may have "jumped the gun." She's also telling me that I should give up smoking.

"I quit when I married George. He made me."

"The brute. . . . Is it Georgina you're worried about?"

"I always worry about Georgina. In relation to this, you mean?" Lena spreads her arms and long hands, a gesture that encompasses her, me, the bed. "No, it's not that." Lena smiles tightly. "Georgina's hardly in a position to criticize me. Considering Elliott. And her behavior. Her general behavior."

"Elliott doesn't seem so bad." Lena groans.

"Anyway," she says, "Georgina probably thinks we've been sleeping together since you got here."

"If only it were so."

"What were you and he talking about this morning anyway?"

"I don't know." I shrug. "The Sex Pistols. Lou Reed."

"Elliott's only conversation."

"Not true. He was also telling me about being in an isolation tank. Sensory deprivation sort of thing."

"Did you notice what horrible teeth he has? All jagged."

"So are mine." I open my mouth wide. As Lena leans over to peer inside, she lets the quilt slip from her full, slightly sloping breasts, freckled and very pale below her tan line.

"Not as jagged as his. . . . It ruins your facial structure."

"What?"

"Smoking. You should really quit. . . . They're going to Santa Barbara together for a horse show this weekend. Georgina's competing and Elliott offered to drive the trailer. I don't like the idea, but I suppose it's better than them riding on his bike. I'd drive her up myself if I didn't have to be at Saint Emydius on Sunday. Want to come along if I decide to go for the day on Saturday? You'll still be around then, won't you?" Lena runs a lacquered nail along my forearm.

"They let Georgina ride with blue and pink hair?"

"She sprays it black for competition and wears a hat." I extinguish the cigarette, reach out and tug at a single strand of hair growing on Lena's right breast. I circle the long thread around her jutting nipple, then take the nipple between my thumb and index finger. Lena arches back her chest and groans.

"Beauty and the beast," I say.

"Yeah? Which is which?" I feel Lena's right nipple grow rigid beneath my touch and watch as her left nipple also puckers, stiffens. I run my free hand down her belly, pulling away the quilt. When I dig my fingers into the thick hair of her groin, Lena reaches down, tries to pull away my hand.

"No. Not again. We need to sleep."

"Later." I shake my hand free from her grasp, slide a finger inside her. Two fingers. Three.

"No."

"I want to make you beg."

"Cal."

"Stay put." Continuing to work her nipple with my right hand, I crawl down, spread tanned thighs, inhale the smell of her sex again greedily. I touch the tip of my tongue to her clit, lap the swelling flesh, slowly and teasingly at first, then more and more rapidly. Lena's body begins to quiver. I find her other breast and, with arms stretched above me, crush both nipples beneath my fingers as I sink my teeth gently into carmine flesh. Lena cries out. I pull back my head, watch her moving above me. Her long amber hair falls across the pillow like waves, her perfect teeth press into her lips, her closed eyelids and sunbleached lashes flutter slightly. I bury my face again, nose and cheeks pressing into moist hair and flesh, mouth and lips sucking Lena's wetness. And probably the residue of my own wetness, but no matter.

"Beast . . . beast . . . beast," Lena says with the soft Southern drawl that I love.

· — · — · — · **43** · — · — · — ·

"YOU REALLY SHOOK them up today," says the priest as he sets down a silver tray containing a plate of croissants, an aluminum pot with coffee, an old-fashioned pressed-glass creamer with matching sugar bowl, paper napkins, plastic spoons, and four red ceramic mugs. Lena did indeed shake them up. When she launched into the discordant opening notes of a Charles Ives piece for organ, a collective murmur rose from the crowd. Sitting on a folding chair beside the organ, I leaned to peer over the balcony railing but quickly ducked back when I saw a mass of startled faces staring up at me. I tried to catch Lena's eyes to fathom her reaction to the small sensation she was creating, but she was completely absorbed in work, fiercely mediating between the sheets of music before her and the heavy keys beneath her hands. Apparently one of Lena's reasons for agreeing to fill in this summer for the troubled organist was that the music-loving priest, Monsignor Conklin, allows her to play whatever pieces she wants for services, including "advanced" ones, although I suspect that most of the parishioners of the Church of Saint Emydius in Rancho Park would not apply that particular adjective.

"Did you like it?" Lena asks.

"Very much so," says Monsignor Conklin, showing dimples above a reddish goatee, "very much so." Lena nods, pleased. During the break between the 10:30 and 12:15 masses, we're having coffee with the monsignor, whom Lena has described as "one of my best friends in Los Angeles." After handing mugs to Lena and me, the priest excuses himself and crosses to a white-haired old woman resting on a sofa at the opposite end of the rectory's long, narrow sitting room. We watch as Monsignor Conklin gently shakes the woman. Getting no response, he pulls what looks to be a bottle of poppers from his jacket and sticks it under her nose. Immediately alert, the old woman has a brief, animated exchange with Monsignor Conklin, then she rises and favors Lena and me with a smile. As the priest leads the tiny, straight-backed figure toward us, Lena whispers that the woman is Monsignor Conklin's grandmother. And, Lena adds, she's ninety-four years old. Where, I whisper, does Monsignor get the amyl? Lena gives me a disgusted look and says that she imagines he gets it from a physician.

When the priest introduces me to his grandmother, I notice that her handshake is firm, her voice sharp and steady, her blue eyes very clear. She certainly doesn't look ninety-four. She playfully raps Monsignor Conklin on the shoulder when he starts to introduce Lena and says that no introduction is needed, she remembers Lena and the trip the three of them made together perfectly well.

"To that rather amateurish—pardon me for being

critical—version of *Faust,* performed in, for goodness sake, *a high school auditorium* in that dusty town. Bakersfield wasn't it, Mrs. James?" Lena confirms that the dusty town was Bakersfield and concurs in Mrs. Conklin's critical judgement of the production.

"It was a concert version," Monsignor Conklin explains to me, "performed by a college group."

"So it was in a *college* auditorium then, Michael?"

"Yes." Mrs. Conklin stirs two cubes of sugar into her coffee.

"What I most remember about that trip," she says meditatively, "was the highways we traveled." The monsignor and Lena exchange glances while we wait for Mrs. Conklin to continue. "Incredibly beautiful structures. One of the true architectural wonders of the world, although I realize they're not commonly recognized as such." Lena tells Mrs. Conklin that I studied architecture.

"Do they teach you to build highways in school?"

"Not really."

"They should. What school?"

"Yale."

"Good school. But you need to know about highways. Then you should go out and build some. But first you'll have to find yourself some Italians."

"Italians?" I ask.

"Don't you know that the Italians are the ones who built the highways? They deserve some sort of medal."

"Italians built the highways in California?"

"Not just in California. Everywhere. The highways were all built by Italians. The president's always handing out medals, but if he really wanted to do some good he'd give medals to the Italians."

"Why Italians?"

"Because they built the highways."

"No, I mean why did the Italians build the highways?" Mrs. Conklin looks puzzled, squints so hard that her wrinkled skin almost closes around her blue eyes. "What troubled me about that trip," she finally says, "were all the dead animals on the side of the road." She shudders.

"You mean on the road to Bakersfield?" Monsignor Conklin asks.

"It was just too upsetting for me, Mikey."

"No, Grandma, I explained to you then that those weren't animals. Just refuse. Occasionally the tires of those big trucks, the semis, blow out. What you saw were big pieces of rubber."

"Really?" Mrs. Conklin stares intently at her grandson, then suddenly her wrinkled face breaks into a smile. "Yes, you did say that. I'm sorry. It's the blood," she explains to Lena and me, "sometimes it doesn't reach my head." The old woman laughs, as though agreeing to forgive a great joke that's been played on her.

Monsignor Conklin wants to know if Lena's had a chance to listen to the Berio album he gave her. I don't know the Berio album and wouldn't understand the musical intricacies Lena and the priest are discussing if I did. I study the rather shabby sitting room with its worn Danish modern furniture and look through dust-streaked French doors on my left to a small, sunny garden. The flowers there, pansies and sweet peas, petunias and asters and geraniums, are all various shades of purple, and I wonder if the color-coordinated plantings are meant to be religiously symbolic. I think of Aunt Em and all of her violets and look back into Mrs. Conklin's face. She meets my gaze, shakes her head angrily.

"There were animals all along the side of the road," the old woman says, "dead and dying, driven out of their homes in the hills by the developers." She spits out the last word, as though uttering a curse. There are tears in her eyes.

I'M IN AN apartment, my apartment on Channon Road in New Haven I think, or maybe Max's apartment off Castro in San Francisco. Yes, it is Max's place, beige and characterless and at the moment very quiet. I'm standing in what must be the passage between the living room and the bedroom, there's a white door to my left, an identical door to my right, and I'm facing a man I've never seen before. The thing about the man is this: He looks completely, almost comically, average. He could be anywhere between thirty and forty-five. He's neither tall nor short, neither fat nor thin. His medium-length, light brown hair tops a face that's neither ugly nor handsome, dark nor light, stupid nor exceptionally intelligent. He wears corduroy pants, a tan cotton dress shirt that's unbuttoned at the neck, brown Oxfords.

Grayish-blue eyes hold, compel really, my own gaze, as the man and I face each other in some sort of silent and motionless combat. Then slowly, almost imperceptibly at first, the man begins to move, but to move without any visible effort on his part, as though he was standing on a turntable. It's only after he's completed a forty-five-degree turn and stands before me in profile that I realize the man is missing a limb. His left arm's gone, but gone recently, for a hole encrusted with dried blood gapes where his shoulder and armpit should be. Almost simultaneously I see the missing limb, it's been here all along, lying near us on the carpeted floor. The solitary arm itself shows no traces of blood, still wears the tan Brooks Brothers shirt rolled up to the elbow. Light brown down on the exposed wrist sparkles in a shaft of afternoon sunlight. I know now, of course, that I have pulled the man's arm from its socket. Unspeakable sadness fills the narrow space around me as I hear, from a distance and very faintly, a band playing a Sousa march. Suddenly the man's head turns, as though jerked by a string, and he winks at me and says, "And you thought you were going to grow up and be president!" No, it's my voice, it's I saying, "And you thought you were going to grow up and be president!"

Then the man's underground. I've buried him on the hill near the oil wells, beneath a huge old mimosa tree. Rain falls from a heavy gray sky, beating mercilessly across my back, gusting into my face. Oh God, I've made a terrible mistake! Through water-blurred eyes I watch as rivulets cascade down the hill, carrying with them sodden pink blossoms that have fallen from the trees and, more importantly, big clumps of red dirt. Doesn't anyone understand! If the rain doesn't stop soon, it's going to uncover the man. I think I can already glimpse the body's outlines beneath the mud. They'll see! For my home, the old gray farmhouse, looms behind the mimosa tree, and people are peering from its darkened windows. I can't make out the faces, but I know that they're there, watching me from behind dirty lace curtains, watching and waiting . . .

And I awake to Lena calling that breakfast will be ready in ten minutes.

I WATCH THE thin man try and fail to hit on a thirtyish blonde sitting alone at the bar. A few minutes later he grabs the only other woman in the room, a pert young waitress, and whispers something into her ear. The waitress good-naturedly struggles out of his grasp. He grins at her, conceding defeat, lurches toward a group of teenage boys. He watches them play video games for a while, then comes over to my table, sets down his drink.

"May I?" the thin man asks. I shrug. He pulls up a chair. I suppose he's joined me, because, aside from the blond woman and the video players and a couple of guys at the pool table in back, I'm the only other customer in the bar tonight.

"What are you drinking?"

"Jack Daniel's."

"It's rum over ice for me, with just a touch of lime. Although," he says, gesturing toward the waitress, "little Susie just told me that I could use more *lime*." He lets out a horsey guffaw.

The supergraphics on the walls of the waterfront bar look like they were painted in the sixties, geometric swirls of orange and yellow and blue, now dirty and faded; and the man opposite me looks like he's from the sixties too. His long black hair almost touches his shoulders, a handlebar mustache curves down his creased cheeks. Faded jeans, a heavy gold chain around his neck, and a red and white floral-printed shirt complete his time-warp appearance. He looks into my face with intent black eyes.

"You know what I think?" he asks rhetorically. "People ought to pay more attention to video games."

"What?"

"Think about it, my friend. What you've got in some of these games is an absolutely perfect graphic representation of the human condition. Don't you see the battle between the individual and his environment? Man constantly fighting off the hostile forces around him? And what makes the games—if you want to call them games—really right on the mark is that no matter how many victories man wins, in the end things always turn out badly for him."

"And what about women?" The thin man laughs.

"You're okay, friend. Now women, they're a whole different story."

Floodlights blaze brightly in the front courtyard, but when I open the door, I step into a darkened house. I make out a faint glow at the end of the hall and follow it to find Lena sitting at the counter between the dining room and the kitchen. A single spot shines directly down on her, encasing her in a cone of white light amidst the surrounding blackness. Lena turns her cheek away when I bend to kiss her, her body stiffens in my embrace.

"What's the matter?" Lena doesn't answer, just looks at me coldly. I study her face, but it offers no clue as to what's bothering her. I turn on some kitchen lights, pour myself a bourbon over ice. I ask Lena if she wants me to make her a drink too.

"Haven't you had enough?"

"What do you mean?" She continues to look at me coldly. She flicks her tongue inside her cheek. "For Christ's sake, Lena, I've had one drink tonight, two. What's wrong with you?"

"Where have you been?"

"I felt like going out to get a drink."

"Where?"

"I don't know. Someplace down the highway. The Malibu something or other. What are these questions?

Is that what this is about? You said you'd be late at rehearsal, so I went out for a drink. You think I should wait around for you all evening?"

"I got home at eleven-thirty. I've been sitting here in the dark for an hour. What was I supposed to do?"

"Well, you could have turned on some goddamn lights for starters."

"You were out, Georgina's *still* out, an hour and a half past curfew. Isn't it enough that I have one child to worry about?"

"Oh, for Christ's sake."

"How could you be gone till twelve-thirty if you only had one drink?"

"I told you I had two drinks." Lena puts her left hand on her temple, rolls back her head in theatrical agony. "You want to know exactly what I did tonight, Lena, is that it? I went to a bar down the highway, I had two, count 'em, two drinks, I watched people play video games, I talked to a drunk. Got that? Then I walked on the beach and then I came home. Got it all?"

"Was the bar . . . ?"

"It wasn't a gay bar, if that's what you're going to ask. And even if . . ."

"Oh stop it! I wasn't . . ." We hear the roar of Elliott's Harley-Davidson in the driveway. Lena abruptly gets off the bar stool, disappears down the hall. I hear her open the front door, then I hear voices raised outside in the courtyard. Is Lena yelling at her daughter because she's mad at me, or was she mad at me because she was worried about Georgina, or both. The front door slams shut, the motorcycle roars away, angry footsteps ascend the stairs, voices above me are raised again, more doors are slammed.

By the time I finish my drink, the house is quiet. As I pass Lena's bedroom door, I notice that she still has her light on. A signal to me, perhaps? If so, I ignore it. In my own room, I undress, get into bed. After fifteen minutes of tossing and turning, though, I throw off the sheets, grab the white terrycloth bathrobe that used to belong to Lena's husband. In the hall a thin line of light still glows beneath Lena's door. I knock lightly. Getting no response, I carefully open the door—I don't want to wake Lena if she's fallen asleep already. She hasn't fallen asleep, she's not even in bed. I find her sitting in the sauna next to her dressing room. When I tap on the little glass window to get her attention, Lena chooses to ignore me. I drop the robe to the floor, step into the heat.

"Get out."

"Let me be with you, Lena."

"I want to be alone."

"I want to stay."

"You want to stay? *Stay.* I'll go out, lock you in here, turn up the heat. I'll let you fry."

"Maybe I wouldn't mind frying . . . If you were with me."

"You're not even supposed to be in my bedroom." Lena closes her eyes on me, but at least she makes no attempt to leave. We sit in tense silence, she on the wooden bench, I on the step below her. I watch rivulets of sweat roll slowly down her freckled, already glistening skin, feel my own body begin to moisten from the waves of heat.

"I'm sorry if I upset you, Lena. Did you think I'd gone?" She doesn't move, doesn't open her eyes. A bead of moisture falls from the tip of her nose onto her lower lip.

"I checked your room when I first got home to see if your things were still here," she says at last.

"I wouldn't leave like that."

"There's so much we don't know about each other, Cal, so much we haven't said."

"I wouldn't leave like that."

"No . . . I don't mean . . ." She shakes her head. "Do you love me?"

"I don't know if I've ever said that to anyone." Lena opens her eyes, finally looks at me.

"You're so young."

"Does that matter?"

"Of course it does." She rubs a palm across her lips. "Come here." I move closer to Lena. She runs her fingers through my damp hair. Then she bends toward me, and a warm breast grazes my cheek. When she cups my balls in her hand, my sex, already heavy from the heat, rises. I'm intoxicated by her touch now, by her wet skin, her wet hair, by the pure smell of the cedar, the sheltering heat.

"I want to fuck you with sweat running down your body," I whisper. "I want our sweat to mix, I want us to come sweat." Lena eases her glistening body onto mine.

"I HATE SUNDAY nights," Georgina announces.

"Why?"

"I don't know. Sundays always seem so sad." She switches on the television with remote control and gets Mike Wallace asking a portly man if he's aware that millions of dollars worth of arms are being sold to Libya through the French subsidiary of the company the man heads. Before the executive can answer, Georgina flicks the channel, then flicks it again and again and again until she's run through all the stations in rapid succession. "Never anything on TV on Sunday," she says, turning off the set.

"Where's Elliott?" I ask. Georgina frowns. She's sprayed her hair with a mix of Monet colors today, lavender, pale blue, rose, and celadon frame her pale, momentarily troubled face. "Something up between the two of you? I haven't seen him around this week."

"As I'm sure Ma has noted with delight. He was here on Wednesday when you were on the beach. Not that it's any of your business." Georgina's Siamese cat pads into the library during the silence, the click of his claws surprisingly loud against the parquet floor.

"Here, Alexander!" Obediently the fat Siamese jumps into his mistress's lap, allows himself to be stroked. I ask Georgina if she wants to play cards.

"I don't know any card games."

"I'll teach you poker then."

"I don't want to learn."

"Why?"

"I have a compulsive personality. I don't think I should take up gambling."

"For Christ's sake, Georgina, you're not going to become a compulsive gambler learning to play poker. One game."

"With people like me, you never know. It's a risk I'd rather not run."

"I certainly don't want to corrupt you."

"I'm already corrupted."

"I doubt that."

"Did you know that Elliott and I didn't stay with the Moores that weekend we went to Santa Barbara? Ma's friends? We rented a motel room instead."

"So?"

"So I couldn't stand being with him for twenty-four hours a day. The only relief was when I was in the ring. I was looking forward to the weekend, but Elliott just got on my damn nerves. I don't know how people can stand being together all the time."

"They adjust, I guess."

"Is that supposed to be your advice?"

"I wasn't aware that I was giving advice."

"Besides, Elliott took up with these really strange people we met in a bar. A girl who thought she was David Bowie. I mean, she dresses like Bowie, has her face made up like his, has her hair cut like Bowie's, she's even listed in the phone book as Bowie. Crazy."

"Perhaps *crazy* is a bit strong."

"This same girl casts horoscopes. She did mine. Elliott insisted. She said that I was in danger of becoming a human vegetable. I don't really believe in astrology, but I figured that if it is true, then being a human vegetable is just the flip side of being compulsive. Sort of yin and yang, you know?" I tell Georgina that I believe in neither astrology nor yin and yang. I ask her if she wants to dance.

"You and me and Ma?" She grins wickedly.

"Yeah sure, why not?"

"Because Ma only dances to the Supremes." She rolls her eyes heavenward. "I mean, really!" Georgina tosses the cat to me, rises and goes to the cabinet that holds the stereo equipment and the television set. She runs her right hand slowly along a row of video cassettes, pulls one out. "If you're so bored," she says, turning to face me, "we could watch one of Pa's movies."

"Don't be a bitch, Georgina. Besides, all of your father's movies are shit."

"They used to call them B movies."

"Well now we call them shit."

Later I watch from the sofa as Georgina and Lena move to the beat of "Stop! In the Name of Love." Lena swivels her hips and torso, makes expansive gestures with her arms; Georgina keeps her torso still and her arms limp as she jerks her spiky helmet of pastel hair and executes a series of minimalistic but intricate shuffles. Gradually, however, the women begin to pick up each other's rhythms, to imitate each other's moves. Somewhat amazingly mother and daughter are soon coordinating their steps, performing together like members of a well-trained dance duo. As they move toward one another, then away from one another, then back together again to execute perfectly synchronized turns, both women break into broad, triumphant grins. Lena looks my way and gestures.

"Get back up here," she shouts happily above the pounding music, "you can't be tired already!"

"Not until you put on something else besides the Supremes," I yell back. Catching Georgina's eye, I wink.

QUITE OFTEN I walk the beach at night. This evening a strong wind blows spray into my face, and icy foam covers my bare feet, laps halfway up my calves. The coast is fogless, and the crashing waves sparkle in the light of a half moon, as though a million tons of glitter had been poured into the sea. The roar of the water seems to create a silence, stark and absolute, and it's in this paradoxical silence that I often feel as though I'm standing at the end of the world. I think, perhaps inevitably, of walking into the ocean and never coming back. I tempt myself with the thrill and relief of oblivion.

But I turn away from the brilliant night water and look down the beach to an opposing and no doubt equally sentimental image: that of the house where I now live. Its rooms glow against the blackness of the mountains and the sky, as clearly defined behind glass walls as the rooms in a dollhouse. I see Lena move across the living room, bend down. Perhaps she's laying a fire or retrieving a sheet of music that's fallen to the floor. In any case I know she's there waiting for me. In any case I know that when I return to the house I'll find light, and food and wine and music, and a daughter, a cat, a pale blue bed. In any case I'll hear Lena's cracker drawl and her honeyed laughter. In any case I'll hold her sharp-boned, hungry body next to mine. In any case.

Of course, it's never as simple as that. Lena rises from the bed. As she bends to pick up a robe, her body looks strangely monumental against the soft glow of the room. Watching the curve of pale buttocks, the slope of dark shoulders, the cascade of wild hair, I'm suddenly pierced with a sad terror of . . . what?

•—•—•—• **48** •—•—•—•

LENA TAPS ON the glass door, slides it open, says that
the phone's for me. For me? Who could possibly be on
the line? No one knows, or no one is supposed to
know, that I'm staying here.

"Do you know who it is?"

"No. Some woman." Lena shrugs. I follow her from
the deck into the living room where a Mozart piano
piece is playing on the stereo. The book that Lena's
been reading for a week, *Henry and Cato,* lies face
down on a table beside a tiny white phone. I tell Lena
that I'll take the call on the extension in the kitchen.

"Hello."

"Hi, Cal." There's a click as Lena replaces the
receiver in the living room.

"Karina." Pause. "How'd you know I was here?"

"I guess that you're delighted to hear from me,
huh?" Pause. "I certainly didn't find it out from you."
Hurt.

"Well," I finally say, "what's up?" Lame, I know.

"What's up? I wanted to see what happened to you. I've been *worried*. People don't disappear every day of the week." Angry.

"I'm sorry. I just needed to . . . hell, I don't know. . . . You must have got my note?"

"Sure. And I quote, 'Thanks for everything. Love, Cal.' Beginning and end of note." Long pause.

"How'd you find out I was here?"

"From Ricky Blumenthal." Lena must have told him. "Lena told him you've been staying with her." Well, why shouldn't she? I didn't ask Lena to keep my being here a secret. Silence as I try to think of what to say.

"Look Cal, maybe I shouldn't have called."

"Maybe not."

"What have I done?"

"What?"

"What did I do to you to make you treat me this way? Did I offend you somehow?"

"No."

"Fuck you."

"Karina, please. I don't want a hassle."

"Fuck you." She's shouting. "You could at least have let me know you were still in town." Pause.

"Actually I'm not. In town I mean, I'm at the beach."

"I've heard all about your beach idyll. Apparently Lena offers glowing descriptions."

"We're happy."

"How quaint! What about the accident?"

"What accident?"

"The reason I've been so frantic is that this man

came by looking for you last week. Said you'd been in some sort of accident." I hold my breath, then speak very slowly.

"What kind of accident did he say I'd been in, Karina?"

"A car wreck or something. He said he had to find you, something about insurance. What happened? Were you hurt?"

"No. . . . What did the man look like?" Karina describes a middle-aged man, tall, dark-haired, handsome.

"Did he have acne scars on his face?"

"Yes. So you know him?"

"What was he wearing?"

"A suit I guess. A light-colored summer suit." Pause. "Cal?"

"Karina, *this is important,* did you tell him I was staying with Lena?"

"How could I? I didn't know then. I just found out from Ricky this morning."

"Did the man give you his name?"

"I can't remember. I don't think so. And he didn't leave a card or anything, which I thought was strange."

"Karina, if he comes back *do not,* I repeat *do not* tell him I'm here."

"All right, all right. But what's going on? What kind of trouble are you in?"

"I'm not in trouble." I have to improvise. "It was just this motor crash-up. I mean, not a crash-up. I hit the man's car pulling out of a parking space. He threatened to sue me, you know? One of those litigious personalities? So I'm trying to avoid him."

"But he said he was an insurance man."

"Well maybe he is. Look Karina, I'm all right. I really am, but I've got to go now."

"Cal—"

"I'll call you in a few days. I really will."

"Cal."

"Bye." I hang up the phone and sag against the oak counter, mindlessly running my fingers along its copper top.

Lena looks up from *Henry and Cato* to ask who was calling when I pass through the living room.

"My friend Karina." I move to the deck and close the glass door behind me before Lena can say anything more. I can't talk to her now.

I have to leave here, leave Lena.

As I walk to the rail the redwood is warm beneath my bare feet.

The last few weeks have been an attempt to forget what can't be forgotten. I realize now. My mistake. My delusion.

The sky is cloudless this afternoon, the ocean is languid, turquoise flecked with purple.

Another delusion: that I've been honest with Lena. She doesn't know that I killed a man with alabaster skin. Nor does she know that I first came to her because I was on the run, or that I'm being chased by an acne-scarred detective who sooner or later—most likely sooner—will catch me. I have to leave Lena before that happens. I'm not sure how much of my panic now comes from fear that Richard Garr will find me here and how much comes from fear that Lena will learn the truth.

Two middle-aged men in bathing suits stroll across

the sand below me, holding hands, trailed by a brown and white beagle. One of the men waves at me.

What can I say to Lena now? A note—a note reading, "Thanks for everything, love, Cal"—hardly seems sufficient. But what would a sufficient valedictory in this case be? What new lies would suffice?

Glimmers of green shoot up from the bottom of the ocean to mix with the shimmering turquoise and purple at the surface.

"We've always known," I'll say, "that this was temporary. What you and I . . ."

I hear the door slide open behind me. Lena steps onto the deck.

"Cal, are you all right?" I turn. Lena's eyes, the green of the ocean's depths, are narrowed and troubled, her mouth is upturned in a questioning smile. She knows the answer to her question.

I jump as the phone rings again.

Lena puts her hands on my bare chest, but I step away from her touch and nod in the direction of the insistently ringing phone.

"That may be Karina again. Please tell her that I can't come to the phone?"

"Why?" I don't answer and Lena goes back into the living room, finally picks up the phone. The wall of glass between us, and the Mozart tape, and the hum of the ocean drown out her voice. I watch Lena, as though I'm studying, trying to memorize the details of a full-length portrait that I may not see again: She balances herself, in a characteristic stance, on her left hip, with her right knee slightly bent, her right foot resting against her left ankle; she gestures with a long musician's hand and runs it through her tousled, amber-colored hair; the lines of her body, clothed today in clinging navy blue, stand out in relief against the bare white wall above the fireplace.

I decide that it must not be Karina on the line after all.

Lena hangs up the phone, stands staring down at it. Finally she looks up and comes toward me. When she steps back onto the deck and sunlight hits her face, I see that she's pale beneath her tan, that the usually unnoticeable lines around her eyes and mouth now look deeply etched. It's as though Lena has aged years in just the last few minutes. Her expression is unfamiliar and unreadable.

"Lena, what is it?"

"Get dressed." Her voice is both icy and edged with hysteria.

"Who was that?"

"The police." She savagely digs a clenched fist into her cheek. "Get dressed. Get your car." I just stare at her.

"What did they say?" I finally ask.

"Georgina . . ." Lena has difficulty speaking. "Georgina's hurt." She gulps out the words. "She's been in an accident."

"Good God."

"A motorcycle accident." Lena leaves a large white patch of skin when she takes her hand away from her face. "She was thrown from Elliott's motorcycle. Against a car."

"But . . . is she . . . ?"

"She's bad. I don't know. They wouldn't say anymore. I know she's bad. They said to get to the hospital immediately."

I reach out, fold Lena's tense body against me.

"Get dressed," she says, "please just get dressed."

·—·—·— 49 ·—·—·—

TWENTY-EIGHT SLEEPLESS hours later we watch as two nurses and a surgeon wheel a bed containing Georgina into an elevator. Fragile, broken, heavily bandaged, she's being taken from the intensive care unit on the second floor up to the kidney dialysis machine on the fifth. Shiny steel doors slide shut behind Georgina and her attendants as Georgina's mother finally breaks.

"What are fish to me?" Lena asks loudly and gestures toward a lithograph depicting two huge red guppies swimming in a bowl of lavender water.

"And what are birds?" She points to another boldly colored print on the opposite wall.

"Lena, let me take you home. You need some sleep."

"No."

"Cal's right," Monsignor Conklin says, "there's nothing you can do here while Georgina's upstairs."

"What is Cal to me?" Lena says, her voice escalating. A man and a teenage boy coming down the corridor look toward us then quickly avert their eyes; a bearded man in a white coat coming out of intensive care also looks toward us but does not avert his eyes. Monsignor Conklin and I exchange glances over Lena's head. He grimaces and raises his sandy eyebrows in a facial shrug.

"Lena dear, please," Monsignor Conklin says when Lena points to a third lithograph, one of an orange and blue striped zebra. He gently places his palm on her shoulder, but Lena jerks away from the good priest. She also jerks away from me, and she begins shaking her head back and forth. The bearded man in the white coat, presumably a physician, approaches. The three of us watch Lena continue to shake her head, in more and more of a frenzy, her amber hair slashing the air and covering her face. Out of the corner of my eye I see Monsignor Conklin nod at the doctor, who, in a flash, steps forward and slaps Lena hard. The sound of the blow echoes in the sterile corridor. Lena reels back, then stands rigid before us. She draws her fingers through her hair, pulling it away from her eyes, and stares down at the linoleum floor.

"I'm sorry," Lena finally says in an affectless voice. She glances up at the doctor. "My daughter is sick." *My daughter is sick!* In fact Georgina is being treated for severe muscle injury, for a lacerated spleen, and for two broken legs. As a result of trauma she also suffers from "acute tubular necrosis" or kidney failure, which, if not reversed within the next few days, will kill her.

50

I FIND LENA sitting on the back steps that lead down to the beach. The night is appropriately black, moonless, and a high tide roars beneath the fragile house, laps at the wooden pilings, almost reaches the rung on which Lena's feet rest.

"You couldn't sleep either," she says.

"No." I sit on the step beside her. "The pills didn't work?"

"No. . . . I envy Monsignor Conklin. I wish that I was religious." She takes my hand. "Maybe I could pretend for tonight. Do you think I could, Cal?"

"I don't know."

"No, no use pretending, I suppose." She laughs a mirthless laugh. "If there is a God, he'd know."

"I don't think he'd mind. . . . Lena, I wish . . ."

"No, Cal, don't say anything. Just sit here with me. . . . It's like a cave down here, isn't it? Water rushing in, almost soothing. . . . I don't know what I'll do if she dies."

"She won't die."

"She could." Yes, she could.

"Lena, if only I—"

"There's nothing any of us can do now, except the doctors, and probably not even them. . . . You're here."

"I love you."

"You look out at the ocean, and you realize how small you are. . . . You didn't see the ocean until you were seventeen, did you, Cal?"

"No, I never saw the ocean."

"Georgina was a baby on the ocean. A California child . . . A bolt from the blue, Cal . . . She has to be all right."

"She will be. We'll all be okay."

"She's a California child. We raised her to be a beautiful California child."

"HOW'S THE BOY?" George James asks when I join him at a table in the hospital cafeteria. George always refers to Elliott as "the boy." Lena does not refer to him at all and disapproves of my visiting him. I sometimes think that in their minds I've become identified with Elliott, but, of course, only I see my psychological and circumstantial kinship with him.

"He's guilty," I say.

"Of course he's goddamn guilty."

"I don't mean he's guilty, responsible. I mean he feels guilty."

"He should. Little bastard was probably on drugs." George squeezes lemon into a Styrofoam cup of tea. I've already learned not to defend Elliott and so once again refrain from pointing out to George what, in any case, he already knows. Elliott may or may not have been "on drugs," but the highway patrol says that if he hadn't swerved his bike to avoid plowing into the car that went out of control on the Pasadena Freeway, both he and Georgina would probably both be dead now, instead of, respectively, scarred for life and near death. George and Lena, however, prefer their interpretation, which casts Elliott in the role of villain. I suppose that in the matter of affixing blame, they don't at this point draw much of a distinction between their daughter dead and their daughter dying.

"What do the two of you talk about anyway?"

"Elliott can't talk." What I don't tell George is that every day Elliott writes out a question for me on a notepad, always the same question: How is Georgina? No change, I told him today, not mentioning that her chances of surviving grow slimmer and slimmer.

"So what do you do up there?"

"I take him magazines. This morning I met his mother and sister. They've been driving down·every day from Garden Grove."

"Up." George ostentatiously motions with his left

arm, waving away the smoke from my cigarette. "You don't drive down from Garden Grove, you drive up."

"Up then. His sister looks like Elliott. Or the way he used to look."

"Kid can have plastic surgery."

"They don't have a lot of money."

"You're a regular Friar Laurence, aren't you?"

"What role would you rather I play?" George adjusts his black-framed glasses, looks me up and down.

"Lena says that you just did the male lead in *Miss Julie.* Seems like pretty good casting to me."

"The analogy I suspect you're making is not entirely apt." And is, of course, deliberately insulting.

"Perhaps not. Sorry."

"I don't know if sorry's good enough, George."

"Christ you're touchy! Forget I said it, okay? I *am* sorry. Lena said that if it wasn't for you she wouldn't have made it through those first couple of days. I'm grateful." George has said this to me before.

"No need for you to be grateful." I've said this to George before.

"I think there is."

"Are Lena and Helen still up in intensive care?"

"Georgina was sleeping, so Lena went home to get a couple of hours rest herself. She'll be back for the dialysis. Helen's still up there." By "home" George means his condominium on Wilshire. Since he flew in from London on Wednesday, Lena has been staying with him there, which is closer to the hospital than the beach house is. Helen, Lena's diminutive, gray-haired, soft-spoken mother, also flew in on Wednesday, from Jackson, Mississippi. Helen has been staying with me at the beach. If George thinks that I'm a combination of the social-climbing stud in *Miss Julie* and a malevolent Friar Laurence, what must Helen make of me? Lena distractedly introduced me as "a friend," and I wonder if Helen knows, or even suspects, that I'm her daughter's lover? Helen and I have, of necessity, been spending a lot of time together, but she remains aloof with me, politely formal. Perhaps that means she does know about Lena and me. Or maybe she thinks I'm living at the beach house because I'm some sort of family retainer, and she wants to keep the proper master-servant distance. In fact, I *have* been cooking breakfast for the two of us every morning and chauffeuring Helen to and from the hospital. While a frequent companion of her mother now, I've only seen Lena briefly during the last few days and then always in the company of her mother or her husband or doctors and nurses.

"What's got you down all of a sudden?"

"What?"

"Penny for your thoughts?"

"Truth, George? I'm thinking about how much I miss Lena."

"You sound surprised." I suppose I am surprised. My eyes meet George's. He used to be an English professor, and bespectacled, rumpled, lanky, with graying hair and tightly stretched delicate features, George still looks more like an academic than a movie producer. I wait for him to make another crack, perhaps to say, not entirely unjustly, that I seem jealous of Lena's attention to their dying daughter. Instead George says:

"Yeah, I can relate to that. Lena can really get to you, can't she?"

·–·–·–· **52** ·–·–·–·

THE NEWS COMES on Thursday afternoon, exactly ten days after the accident. George and Lena are waiting in the visitors' lounge to tell us when I bring Helen back from lunch. Lena and Helen embrace, hold one another tightly, then George wraps his long arms around them both. No one speaks for a long time. Finally I ask if Elliott knows yet. I'm standing outside the family circle, and no one seems to hear me.

People speak of reading the look in a person's eyes, but when I sit down beside Elliott's bed, I realize that the eyes alone tell you nothing. Elliott's face, swollen to the size of a small pumpkin and covered with partially bandaged cuts and bruises, is, of necessity, expressionless, and hence so are his eyes— expressionless and puzzling. Following our established ritual, I wait patiently while Elliott takes a pencil and notepad from the bedside table, slowly and painstakingly prints the question, hands the pad to me: "How is Georgina?"

"She's out of danger, she's going to be all right." I repeat my words. Now the dark eyes flicker, and I hear a terrible grinding sound as Elliott attempts to speak through wired jaws. His painful efforts result only in a sibilant rush of breath through missing front teeth and a seemingly disconnected groan. I pick up the pencil and notepad again, but Elliott waves them away, turns his face to the wall. The old man in the next bed who's recuperating from a gall bladder operation goes into a coughing fit. When Elliott turns back to me tears are streaming down his ruined face. He reaches out for me, and as I bend toward him I feel my own face crumble. I lay my head against his heaving shoulder, and together we cry tears of gratitude and relief and joy.

LENA CONFESSES:

"God, I wish George hadn't told you. I probably would have told you myself, but I wanted it to be at the right time, in the right way. Damn him.

"You have to know that it didn't mean anything. Or

rather it *did* mean something, but not in relation to you and me, if you can understand the distinction? George and I were married for sixteen years, after all. We're still married as far as that goes, and that whole history doesn't just disappear. When he came back and Georgina was in the hospital . . .

"Damn, I don't know how to explain. It started the second night after George got back from London. We'd been at the hospital all day long, were dead tired. We ordered out for some food, Chinese, and we drank a lot of wine. And maybe I'd taken some pills, I don't remember, it doesn't matter. We were together again after all those years and George needed me. I'm not sure how it happened, these things just do. I needed him too, wanted him.

"After that things just continued. It somehow seemed natural—or maybe inevitable is a better word —while we were staying here together. I admit that I wasn't thinking about you then, Cal, but that was because you were something completely different, separate, not related to what was happening here at all.

"I never meant to hurt you. That's a standard line, isn't it? But it was as though George and I were living in a world completely our own, living in a cocoon of—what? fear?—waiting to see what was going to happen to Georgina. I don't mean to use Georgina as an excuse, but you do strange things under circumstances like that. Damn, it does sound like I'm making excuses, but I'm only trying to explain.

"I just don't want you to think I'm terrible. I don't feel terrible. You *know* how much I care for you. What happened with George has nothing to do with that. I don't want you to leave, but I do have to stay for a while longer near the hospital. Please understand. You know that George is leaving tomorrow, and what happened between him and me is *already* over."

I look around the alien apartment where I've confronted Lena tonight, a luxurious aerie high above the lights of the city. All beige and brown, leather and travertine, the place disgusts me, makes me imagine the unspeakable life that's lately been led between its walls. I feel as though I'm going to suffocate. Cocoon indeed! And isn't that what all love is, a cocoon against the outside world? Easily pierced. I'm filled with hatred for George, overwhelmed by Lena's nervous recital of her betrayal. I make my way to the door, ignoring Lena's pleas. I can't listen to her anymore, can no longer look upon her now painful beauty.

I'M WALKING THROUGH what in the forties was called a motor court, heading toward a row of small stone cabins with wooden front porches. There's another row of cabins to my right, and to my left a pair of wrought-iron flamingos mark a path into a forest. Men and women whom I don't know, perhaps half a dozen of them, move back and forth among the porches, laughing, chatting, oblivious to my presence. From the cabin directly before me comes the sound of music, slightly menacing, pseudo-oriental music, the kind you hear in forties movies when the main character enters an opium den, perhaps, or climbs the stairs to an apartment in which an enemy is waiting for him. The rickety front porch squeaks as I step onto it, and I awake, awake to a gray and foggy morning.

As I reach for a pack of Camels on the bedside table, I hear the music from the dream again. *What?* Yes, a cluster of jangling, discordant piano notes is definitely coming from somewhere inside the house. Only I'm supposed to be alone here. Helen is back in Jackson, Mississippi, and Lena continues to stay in George's apartment on Wilshire. And I continue to stay on alone here. Waiting for Lena to return. Yes, despite everything, waiting for Lena to return.

I get out of bed and make my way slowly down the carpeted hall, following the strange music. At the open door to Lena's bedroom I stop: The jarring piano notes are coming from inside. Well, maybe Lena came home during the night. Except that the rose and sand-colored room looks empty and the bed, visible from the hallway, clearly hasn't been slept in.

"Lena?" The music suddenly stops. "Lena?" No answer. Cautiously I step into the room, and just then the piano notes ring out again, and I find Alexander, the fat Siamese, walking back and forth across the keyboard of the antique clavichord in the far corner. Drat the cat. When I clap my hands, he jumps down and scurries past me into the hallway. I follow Alexander out, closing Lena's door behind me to prevent any more early-morning recitals.

I smoke my wake-up cigarette, then slip into shorts, a sweatshirt, and running shoes. In the kitchen I find Alexander once again waiting for me. I open a can of Kitty Queen Seafood Treat for him and grind some coffee beans for myself. After making sure that the coffee has begun to drip from the machine, I take the stairway outside the kitchen down to the beach and step into the thick fog. I've begun to run every morning, and I like gray days like this best, I like the sting of the chill ocean air, the tiny drops of moisture that collect on my skin, the sense of running through a gauzy dreamscape. Only occasionally do I meet another jogger, and since I run down near the water, away from the houses, even the lights from the kitchens and bedrooms of other early risers come through the fog with a golden, otherworldly glow. Out here in the mornings I find a peace that is, momentarily at least, genuine.

In the distance a man steps through the fog. I first recognize the distinctive, light-colored cotton suit. As we draw closer, the curly hair, the tanned, strong-boned face, the powerful, slightly sagging body come into focus. I keep running toward him, and as we meet our eyes lock once again, and he raises his thick hand, either to wave or to gesture for me to stop, I'm not sure which. I run past him toward the wavery horizon, don't look back. For a moment or so I hear only the reassuring roar of the ocean, but soon, as I knew I would, I also hear his feet pounding the sand behind me.

"I . . . just . . . want . . . to . . . talk," he gasps as he pulls alongside me. I don't turn my head to look at him, but keep my eyes trained on the vast wetness of sea and sky before me. We run down the beach together for a long while, neither of us decreasing nor increasing his pace. Then he reaches out and grabs my wrist, and simultaneously he stops in his tracks. The impact causes me to stumble and fall to the wet sand at the detective's feet. It's over.

Fall

55

A SMALL SWIMMING pool, its turquoise surface streaked with the white of reflected afternoon light, fills the center of the photograph. The pool is bordered on the right by a patch of lawn that's been burned yellow by the sun, and beyond that a field of bermuda grass stretching to a flat, cloudless horizon. On the left, between the pool and a wood and stucco building in shadow, there's a concrete patio furnished with two green and white plaid plastic lawn chairs, a small imitation wrought-iron table, and a dirty white pool float. On the far side of the pool, at the top of the photographic frame, the patio continues in an L shape, and here there's a diving board and an aluminum and plastic chaise longue. A man lies on the chaise. Clad only in a brief black swimsuit, he's tanned and muscular. His hair is sun-bleached and in need of a trim, and his eyes—my eyes—are closed. Sitting on another imitation wrought-iron table beside me are a brown and yellow plastic bottle of suntan oil, a pack of Camel cigarettes, a cheap glass ashtray half-filled with butts, and a small transistor radio.

I toss the photograph onto two dozen or so other photographs spread across the black Formica table-top.

"And these are the negatives?" I ask, picking up a blue and white envelope. Phillip nods. "And you're sure these are the only ones?"

"That's what Garr said."

"And you trust him?"

"I don't have any reason not to."

"No?"

"Not that I know." Phillip stands in front of the glass doors to the terrace, his lanky frame silhouetted against a bright morning sky and hills dotted with pastel buildings. Eastern sunlight streaming past him into my eyes makes it impossible for me to see the expression on his face. He's probably positioned himself this way deliberately.

I turn my back on Phillip and move to the kitchen sink. I remove the negatives from their envelope, and when I strike a match to the strips of amber-colored plastic, they immediately burst into flames, sending up wisps of black smoke and filling the air with the sickly sweet odor of burning chemicals. I drop the negatives into the sink, where they blaze brilliantly against the white porcelain before crumpling into charred black heaps.

When I turn back to Phillip, he's stacking the photographs into a neat pile on the table.

"Are you going to burn these too?" he asks, too cheerfully, too obligingly.

"Maybe you'd like to keep them, Phillip?" He shakes his head no. "Why did you do it, Phillip?" He shrugs. "Don't goddamn shrug at me. You owe me more of an explanation than that." I can now see Phillip's face, which takes on that helpless, stricken look I've always hated. His bony Adam's apple moves up and down.

"I told you I was worried about you," he says.

"Not good enough."

"I had to find out what happened."

"Why should it concern you?"

"Cal, please—"

"You're self-righteous and you're selfish."

"Maybe so, but I was worried. No one knew what had happened to you, where you were."

"And that gave you the right to have me followed?"

"You left town so abruptly. No one knew where you were. I called Max. I called George Deutsch. No one knew."

"Don't you think people have a right to leave town without explaining it to *anyone?* Don't you think they have a right to disappear forever? Haven't you heard about these people who walk out on their jobs, their wives, their kids, and just vanish? Who made you God? What gave you the right to have me chased down like some goddamn missing dog, like some common criminal?"

"I didn't mean you to think that. You weren't supposed to know."

"Richard Garr is not exactly Mr. Efficiency. I've known for weeks that I was being followed. How do you think that made me feel, Phillip? What would you feel like if you were being chased across the country, followed everywhere you went?"

"I'm sorry for that."

"You're sorry? You're *sorry!* Jesus Christ! You make

my life miserable, turn it into a living hell, and now all you can say is that you're *sorry!*"

"I don't know what else to say." I look into Phillip's infuriatingly sad eyes, then turn away to curb my anger. I've got to calm down if I'm to find out what has really been going on, if I'm to discover how much of the truth Phillip is telling, if I'm to know how safe I am now. I glance around my apartment, which seems both totally familiar and alien, the way places do when you return to them after a long absence. My suitcase sits unpacked near the front door where I left it when I got back last night, and the whole place has an almost palpable residue of its months of emptiness.

"Just tell me this, Phillip, how long had you been having me followed before I left San Francisco?"

"Before you left town?" I watch his face very carefully.

"Yes."

"I don't understand." He does look genuinely puzzled.

"You've been having me followed for months, haven't you? Ever since we broke up."

"No, of course not."

"No?" He didn't have Garr following me before I left town? On the night in June, for example, when I went to a house in the Berkeley hills and murdered a man?

"Why should I have you followed then?"

"Words like *jealousy, possessiveness, voyeurism* come to mind."

"I only hired Garr after you disappeared."

"I don't believe you."

"Why wouldn't you believe me? Ask Garr."

"I never want to see Garr's ugly face again, and why should he tell me the truth? I'm sure the two of you have your stories coordinated."

"I'm telling you the truth. Don't get crazy, Cal."

"You're telling me not to get crazy. That I like. You have me followed for two months, if not more, trailed across the country by a detective, as though we were all living in some goddamn movie, and at God only knows what cost. That's six months, six months after our relationship has ended. *Ended,* Phillip. You think that's *normal?*"

"I still love you."

"He still loves me! *L'amour fou!*" I want to crush Phillip's long neck between my hands. Instead I again ask him how long he was having me followed before I left for Tulsa.

"How many times do I have to say it? I only hired Garr *after* you disappeared. You'll just have to believe me." Yes, unfortunately I suppose I will. "What's the point of all these questions about when I hired Garr anyway?" That, Phillip, you'll never know. Not if I can help it. I lie down on the unmade bed, stare up at the ceiling.

"I want to find out how long you've been crazy, Phillip. Tell me, what did Garr report to you?"

"He told me where you were staying."

"And what I was doing?"

"And what you were doing."

"You got off on that?"

"No."

"I bet you did. You're a real voyeur, aren't you, Phillip? So's Garr."

"Oh Cal."

"You're sick, you know, really sick. I always suspected it, but now I'm sure."

"Stop it."

"The truth hurts, huh?"

"The truth is that I had Garr find you because I was worried about you." Phillip's face reddens with anger. "People get murdered you know." On guard again, I sit up, look at Phillip hard.

"What do you mean by that, 'People get murdered.'"

"You know damn well what I mean."

"I don't." Phillip stares at me, and I wonder if he can see my panic.

"Maybe I'm being overly dramatic," he finally says, "or rather was being overly dramatic when I hired Garr. But I didn't know what to think then. Hell, you know I've always thought what you were doing could be dangerous. I really didn't think you were dead, but—"

"You thought *I* had been murdered?"

"I didn't seriously think that, but it *was* a possibility. You did disappear 'without a trace' as they say. . . . Why are you laughing?" I'm laughing with relief, Phillip, laughing at the hideous absurdity of it all. "Stop laughing that way." I wipe tears from my cheeks, try to think again.

"It doesn't make sense, Phillip. If it was my *life* you were concerned about, why didn't you call off Garr once he found me, once you knew I was alive?"

"Because then you disappeared again."

"So what?"

"What do you want me to say? To admit that I wanted to know where you were going next? Okay, I admit it."

"Did Garr tell you why I left Tulsa?"

"I don't think he knew."

"He knew all right. He didn't tell you what happened in Tulsa?"

"He gave me a record of where you were going, who you were seeing, that sort of thing."

"I left Tulsa the night that Garr and I made it together, Phillip. The night we fucked and the night I found out he was a detective. You didn't know about that, did you? Garr didn't write that up for his report."

"No he didn't." Phillip's voice is flat, neutral.

"You were being conned, Phillip. I wonder if maybe Garr didn't follow me to California because *he* became as obsessed with me as you apparently were. Maybe both of you were obsessed, only he conned you into footing the bill. What do you think of that theory?" Phillip nods noncommittally.

"Well," he says, "you're back," and he grins his lopsided grin. Yes. After my talk with Garr on the beach yesterday, I called Phillip and arranged this meeting, then spent the afternoon and evening driving the flat, desolate stretch of Highway 5 from Los Angeles to San Francisco. Yes, I'm back. I leap from the bed and go after Phillip. He tucks his chin into his chest and throws his arms around his head to ward off my blows. So I pound my fists against his back, beating furiously, mindlessly, over and over again. Trying to get away from me, Phillip bumps against the table and knocks the stack of photographs to the floor. I hold on to his shoulder with my left hand and continue flailing with my right as we lurch about the room. We stagger against the sleeping platform, overturning the reading lamp and knocking the receiver off the phone, then Phillip drops to the floor and rolls himself into a fetal ball. I throw myself on top of him and try to turn him over. The photographs crackle beneath us as we struggle, and finally I manage to flatten Phillip's back against the floor and pry his large, bony hands away from his face.

Then I'm sitting on his chest, with his arms pinioned beneath me, closing my hands around his throat. I watch, mesmerized, as my fingers press deeper and deeper into the soft flesh. I don't know how long it is before I become aware of Phillip's gurgled cries, but it's at that point that I drop my hands and roll off his body. The two of us lie several feet apart, crying softly, panting, trying to catch our breaths, and I remember the first time I saw Phillip. He was wearing a gray flannel suit that night, and a red tie, and a pale blue Brooks Brothers shirt, a shirt just like the one he has on today. He was tall and blond and moved through the crowded party with a lanky, awkward grace. I remember exactly what I thought when he turned his head and saw me looking at him from across the room. He gave me a gorgeous, lopsided grin and I thought: This one's going to be more than a one-night stand.

·—·—·— **56** ·—·—·—·

WHEN RICARDO SITS down at the drafting table in front
of me the back of his gray sweatshirt is streaked with
sweat. At the small architectural firm where I work
now a yoga instructor comes every Tuesday at noon to
give a class, and a dance instructor comes at the same
time every Friday. Like several other employees who
take the "jazz" dance class, Ricardo often works
through Friday afternoons in a leotard and whatever
other sweat-soaked garments he's worn to class. The
dress here is in any case casual. So is the office. Jimmy
Sawyer and Rick Neu, the firm's principals, have
private cubbyholes at the front of the building, but the
rest of us, twelve not counting Jimmy and Rick, all
work in one huge, cement-floored, skylit, second-
story space that used to be a button factory. The
dance and yoga classes are held in the "lounge,"
which also houses a wall of kitchen fixtures and a
Nautilus machine and is the only part of the original
space that's been partitioned off. The plaster Doric
columns and the sheets of pastel-laminated plywood

that separate the lounge from the rest of the space are the only examples here of the firm's architectural "style."

The casual atmosphere and the absence of any visible signs of affluence notwithstanding, Sawyer and Neu is, in fact, admirably professional and, in its own way, quite successful. A surprisingly large number of clients seem to like—in any case they pay for—Rick and Jimmy's synthesis of Gehry-style roughness, high-tech slickness, and camp classicism. Most of our jobs are small, of course, many of them renovations and recyclings. At the moment, for example, I'm working on an interior rendering of an old basement that Rick and Jimmy are converting to a downstairs showroom for a boutique that sells Italian sportswear. The team's decision to leave the basement's concrete walls in their original, mottled state and their placement of a plaster, overscale Roman column beside the staircase are typical. My problem at the moment is the floor. The specs say that it's to be made of bleached oak with slabs of honey-colored marble inset to form a pathlike pattern to the dressing rooms. Since I'm working in black and white, the question is this: Which should be a lighter shade in the drawing, the wood or the slabs of marble?

Suddenly the screechy singing voice of Richard Hell blares out at top decibel. His anthem "Blank Generation" bounces off the cinderblock walls and concrete floor, filling the entire space. I look across the room to see Darcy dancing in a pink leotard and holding a big tape deck, one of those that people seem to find so annoying when kids play them on the buses. Darcy, a recent graduate in architecture from the

University of California at Berkeley, is certainly one of the odder people here.

"Take it down, Darcy!" someone behind me yells.

"Motion seconded!" shouts Ricardo. Darcy lowers the volume but continues, arrogantly, to dance. Blank generation indeed. Blank generation, blank years. Everyone here thinks that I, like Darcy, am "recently out of college," which has the distinct advantage of erasing, in one context at least, several years of my life.

146 Central Park West
New York
October 12, 1978

Dear Cal,

I was glad to finally hear from you. It took me awhile to get your letter, since, as the above address indicates, Georgina and I are now back in New York, and it had to be forwarded.

You'll be happy to know that Georgina's recovery is progressing very nicely. Of course, it all seems painfully slow, and it's not very pleasant for her, to say the least, to be cooped up in the apartment most of the time. Still, we have many blessings to count. A tutor comes in five days a week, and the doctors think that she'll be well enough to return to Dalton next term. I again want to thank you for your concern for Georgina and for your loving patience during those weeks in California when everything looked so bleak.

I do understand, in answer to your question, why you felt you had to leave Malibu when you did, although I wish your departure hadn't been quite so abrupt. You're wrong about George and me, although again, I can understand why you felt as you did at the time. I only wish that you had talked with me about it all before you left. No, George and I are not "together" again, we never were really, just briefly pulled back into our shared past by fear and grief and circumstance. I don't mean to apologize, and I don't mean to sound accusatory when I say that I wonder if you didn't use what happened between George and me as some sort of excuse, knowing that our time together, yours and mine, had gone about as far as it could go, and that our days together were, in any case, numbered?

I'm expressing all of this very badly, but what I really want to say, Cal, is that what we had, the love we shared, was real for me, and, I think— hope—for you. And no less real for being fragile, and as you put it, "perishable." Don't sell us short. As for me, I'm grateful for the time we shared.

I thought of you last week—actually I think of you often, but I thought of you particularly then—

237

when I went to see a small exhibition of paintings by John Singer Sargent. Mostly they were scenes of Venice—canals and buildings and interiors—but I think it was the colors, all rose and deep green and gold, bathed with light, yet shadowy, mysterious— that brought back an intense, painful rush of feeling about you. Or maybe that transient stab of loss I felt thinking about you in the gallery had nothing to do with the paintings at all. Someone said, Proust or Oscar Wilde, I think, that the true paradises are those we have lost. Enough of that though.

Your new job sounds fine, maybe you shouldn't be so cynical about it? I think we musicians are lucky in that we don't have such a long apprentice-ship, and because, unlike architects, we get to see—or rather to hear—the results of our labors immediately, no matter that more often than not we're displeased with those results.

Maybe you could drop me a line occasionally and let me know how the job and everything else is with you? And if you're in New York anytime during the year, please give me a call. The number is listed and I'll be here at least through the spring. I agree that those weeks in California can't, shouldn't be, recaptured, but that doesn't mean we have to become total strangers.

Again, dearest Cal, my gratitude for everything, and my love,

Lena

·—·—· 58 ·—·—·

AN EMPTY THURSDAY evening. I could read, I suppose, or watch TV, but instead decide to take a long shower. I'm luxuriating in warm water and steam when the phone rings. I consider not answering it. The person on the line could well be an interested john. I still get plenty of those calls, from former customers, or men referred by former customers, or men who apparently read back issues of the newspapers where my ad used to appear. After five rings, however, I turn off the tap, grab a towel. I shiver as I step into the chill air—the manager of my building hasn't yet turned on the winter heat.

After I pick up the receiver and recognize Tom Tree's distinctive voice, I wish I hadn't answered after all. Tom, unlike me, hasn't yet exorcised his Oklahoma drawl. I'd rather be warding off horny old men than dealing with him. After a few strained and almost apologetic pleasantries, Tom gets to what I suppose is the point of his call. He says that they're having a party on Halloween Eve and would like me to come. Surprised at hearing from Tom and astounded by his invitation, I'm not quite sure how to respond. Finally I say that I already have plans for that night, a lie. Tom says that he's sorry I can't join them, he's heard that Halloween in San Francisco is wild. I say—coldly—that Halloween in San Francisco *used* to be wild. We have an awkward silence before I tell Tom good-bye. There's really nothing more to say.

As I follow a path of wet footprints back to the bathroom I shiver, and not just from the cold. "They" indeed. Tom arrived from Tulsa only a few days after I returned to the city in August. When he phoned from the Greyhound bus station, I told him that he was welcome to stay with me for a week or so, until he found a job and a place to live. In fact Tom never found either, at least not in the sense that he originally intended.

Phillip was still phoning me four or five times a week when Tom first got here. I refused to speak to Phillip, I'd hang up immediately when I heard his voice, but his calls persisted. Then, after I went to work for Sawyer and Neu, Tom was, of course, often alone in the apartment during the day, and so he began to get Phillip's calls. When he told me about the first call, I instructed him to begin hanging up on Phillip too. Tom, I found out later, didn't follow instructions, and Phillip began chatting him up, originally, I suspect, to pump Tom for information about me. Without my knowing it at the time, the two of them began to develop a telephone friendship. Then they decided to meet face to face, and a couple of weeks after their first meeting, Tom moved in with Phillip. According to Tom, the two of them are "in love," whatever that's supposed to mean, and Phillip is going to support Tom while the latter establishes a "musical career" out here. I hadn't heard from either of them since Tom first told me about their proposed alliance and don't know what to make of the invitation to "their" Halloween party. I suppose it's best to avoid speculating about their motives for inviting me to the party, just as it's best to avoid speculating about their motives—especially Phillip's—for getting involved with one another. Perhaps their relationship has nothing to do with me at all. Perhaps.

KARINA STEPS FROM a black Mercedes limousine while a chauffeur and a doorman unload half a dozen or so pieces of Gucci luggage. Karina wears a white mink jacket over white silk slacks and a blouse that's the violet color of her eyes. Her hair is piled in (fake?) curls atop her head and her face is heavily—almost unrecognizably—made up: ruby lips, pink cheeks, lavender lids above kohl-rimmed eyes. Bellhops rush forward as Karina marches into the hotel's ornate lobby. When the man at the front desk asks her how long she'll be staying, Karina smiles mysteriously and says, "As long as it takes."

Still dressed in the white mink jacket and the white silk slacks, Karina knocks on the front door of a small frame house. An attractive, middle-aged woman answers the door, looks at Karina with what could be fear, then notices the chauffeur and limo waiting at the curb in the suburban-looking neighborhood.

"Mother, you look so surprised," Karina says, bending to kiss the woman who's at least half a head shorter than she.

Later, in a yellow-and-white kitchen, Karina and her mother drink coffee from yellow mugs and talk about Karina's month-long stay in Paris. Her mother says she wishes that Karina would have stayed longer there, it seems to have agreed with her.

"You have a glow," she tells Karina. Karina laughs and says that her glow isn't from being in Paris. Mother looks at daughter anxiously, asks what she's really doing back in town so soon, if returning is such a wise idea? Karina says that she'll have some wonderful news soon, everything will work out just fine. Her mother doesn't seem reassured, but Karina just laughs, then asks if she can have a *real* drink.

In her hotel suite, Karina lounges on a white satin chaise. On a table near her sit a bottle of champagne in a silver bucket and two crystal glasses. There's a knock on the door, and a handsome young man enters. Karina rises to greet him, and the two embrace, not passionately, but tentatively and tenderly. The young man, Peter, tells Karina that he's glad she's home. For the first time she loses her air of hard assurance. Peter asks how Paris was. Karina says that she never should have gone away, she realizes that now. She's come back to Peter and has something exciting to tell him. Peter looks stricken, says that he has something to tell her first—a lot has happened during the last month. A lot happens in any month, says Karina, what specifically? Peter hesitantly tells her that he married Diana last Saturday, they're leaving on their honeymoon tomorrow. Karina's face clouds over, she turns away to hide her deep disappointment. Her bare shoulders tremble above her red chiffon evening gown. Then she pours two glasses of champagne, and, turning back to Peter, puts on a bright smile. I'd hoped, she tells him, that we'd be celebrating something else tonight, but, *c'est la vie,* here's to you and your bride. She raises her glass. I'm sorry, Peter says. Drink up, says Karina.

Later that night Karina drinks the last drop of champagne straight from the bottle. Her face is streaked with mascara, her hair is disheveled, her red chiffon dress is tangled among the bedclothes. A crystal glass lies overturned on the carpet, Seconal capsules are strewn across the nightstand. Karina picks up the telephone, tangling her arm in its cord, loudly tells room service to bring up another bottle of Dom Perignon. When she falls back onto the bed, her black curls spread across the pillow like Medusa's, and she laughs a laugh that is harsh and hysterical.

Wearing a black silk suit and a black straw hat with a white rose pinned to its brim, Karina walks through a door labeled WAYNE COUNTY DISTRICT ATTORNEY. She tells a male secretary that she wants to see Mr. Perot. When the secretary replies that she'll need an appointment, Karina waltzes right past him into the inner office, clicking stiletto heels against a terrazzo floor. The district attorney, tall, dark, and handsome, rises from behind his desk when Karina enters. The secretary who's followed says, "I told her you were tied up . . ." but the district attorney waves away the explanation, tells him to leave the two of them alone.

When the door's closed, the district attorney turns to Karina, glares at her. He wants to know what the hell she's doing back in town? Karina smiles at him seductively, says, what's the matter, Judd, aren't you glad to see me? Judd Perot snorts with disgust, reminds Karina that he paid her a fortune to get away and stay away, and she damn well better live up to her end of the bargain. Karina says that she's decided maybe the bargain wasn't such a good deal after all. Judd says that he's not going to pay her another penny, and, if she's not out of town by tomorrow, he'll reopen the investigation. Karina tells him that he doesn't seem to understand, that the situation has changed somewhat, the two of them have a problem. Judd says that he doesn't have a problem at all, but Karina will certainly have a problem—five to ten years behind bars—if she doesn't do what he says.

"You wouldn't," Karina asks, "send the mother of your own child to jail, would you?"

"You're not . . . ?"

"Oh, but I am, Judd, I am. Three months to be exact." The district attorney's face registers disbelief, then despair. The credits come up on a freeze frame of Karina's triumphant, ruby-lipped smile.

·—·—·—· **60** ·—·—·—·

INDIAN SUMMER SEEMS to linger on indefinitely this year. On the last Sunday afternoon of November the air is clear and balmy, and most of the men gathered on the redwood deck are coatless, with a few of the more dedicated exhibitionists among them also shirtless. The bright blue sky and the distant, verdure-covered hills provide a spectacular backdrop, and the smattering of bare, still tan skin, and the tall turquoise drinks that are the adjoining bar's "specialty," and the reggae beat of Jimmy Cliff from the sound system lend the scene a festive, almost tropical flavor. Large glass doors open from the deck to the bar, flooding the black and silver room with light and fresh air. The bar's other walls, all mirrored, reflect the sky, the men in the sun, and wooden boxes of flowering shrubs, and further dissolve, in classic California fashion, the distinction between indoors and out.

Marty, the mustachioed bartender, sways to the music as he slides two Budweisers across the brushed-steel countertop to Max and me. Our drinks are, as always here, free of charge, presumably in acknowledgment of our value to the establishment as decorative objects, as icons of desirability. I jokingly tell Marty that Max is flush now, he should make him pay, but Marty just smiles and boogies down to some customers a couple of bar stools away. Max sticks out his tongue at me and takes a swig of beer.

"What you realize really quickly," he says, "is that you're on the side of the bad guys. Always." Max is talking about the big downtown law firm where he's working now.

"Always?"

"Nearly always. Most of the time, of course, you're representing a bad guy who's fighting another bad guy, big corporations going after each other. As in the case of *Barracuda* v. *Barracuda.*"

"A guy my brother went to school with is one of the lawyers on the Silkwood case."

"I never knew you had a brother."

"Now you know, and one of my brother's buddies from high school is a lawyer for Kerr-McGee. A bad guy not fighting another bad guy. He's fighting the family of a murdered heroine."

"A heroine? Maybe. Murdered? Perhaps. But that's exactly the way it goes."

"And it doesn't bother you at all that you'll be one of the bad guys?"

"No, no, Cal baby, you don't understand. I'll just work for them." Max flashes me a self-consciously cynical grin. His big teeth gleam.

"You know Max, Kerr-McGee had an enormous refinery about twenty miles east of where I grew up. Did I ever tell you about that? The way the place stunk like hell? When there was a strong westerly wind, the stench blew into town, a smell like rotten eggs, like thousands of goddamn rotten eggs. And many summer nights I lay in bed and that smell came through the screened window beside my bed, filling the room, suffocating me, so . . ." I don't know what I'm trying to say.

"So?"

"So fuck your cynicism."

"Or Cal won't love me anymore?" Max hums along with "The Harder They Come."

"Maybe not." I look into the mirror above the bar, survey the crowd. On the opposite side of the room I see the vaguely familiar face of a young man standing near a huge urn filled with orange-tipped birds of paradise. It can't be.

"What's wrong, Cal?"

"What? Oh . . . nothing." The man in the mirror is short and stocky and has dirty blond hair that's shorter now than it was in any of the photographs I've seen of him. I turn to get a better look. No, there's no question in my mind about who he is.

"A hot one," Max says, having followed my gaze.

"I think I'm going to walk around."

"No problem." Max leers. "Have fun."

The pretty people around me, the reggae beat, the Sunday sun and shadow, all seem to fade and then dissolve as I stare at the young man hiding behind the birds of paradise. Of course, he's not really hiding, and as I move toward him, he meets my gaze with interested, deep-set brown eyes.

"Cal," I say, extending my hand.

"Buddy," he says as his flesh meets mine. Yes, I know.

* * *

There's no easy way to do this. I've put off Buddy's immediate overtures for sex by offering him a beer and a couple of lines of coke. We're sitting on my bed, still dressed, but Buddy's getting restless again. Perhaps a direct approach would be best, although not too direct. I tell him that his face looks familiar.

"Yeah, yours too. I guess we must have seen each other around." His voice still has traces of the rural South—North Carolina, if I remember correctly.

"Where'd you grow up?"

"A little town in South Carolina that you've probably never heard of. Gardenville." Yes, *South* Carolina.

"Have you ever done any modeling?" Buddy looks at me suspiciously, removes his hand from my thigh.

"Why do you ask?"

"I'd swear I've seen a photograph of you recently. I'm trying to remember where."

"I've done some modeling. Yes."

"Where?"

"Hey, what is this, the Spanish Inquisition or something?" Buddy laughs. I don't want to tip my hand too soon. I go to fetch two more Budweisers from the refrigerator. When I return Buddy has removed his shoes and T-shirt and is sprawled across the bed. Looking up at me, he grins and asks if I've got any dirty videos. His front teeth are slightly crooked. I lie to him, say that I wish I did have some porn for us to watch.

"Have you been in any films?" I ask.

"Some." Buddy runs a hand provocatively across his pale, hairless chest, rubs his nipples. "And I've been in some skin magazines, if that's what you're getting at."

"I saw a photograph of you in the newspaper a

couple of months ago, Buddy." After I've said it, I hold my breath, waiting for his reaction. He sits up slowly, his face goes slack, and for a long time he just stares at me dumbly. Then he rises from the bed, jabs his fist through the air, as though he's punching at some invisible opponent.

"Christ," he says, "I knew that was going to fucking ruin me in this town."

"Why?"

"What do you mean why? You said you saw the photograph in the paper. You ought to know."

"You were accused of murder, weren't you?"

"And you knew that when you brought me here?" he asks incredulously.

"No, I knew I'd seen your face somewhere before, but I just now remembered the photograph in the newspaper and the story."

"Well, it was all a pack of fucking lies." He looks at me, his expression both helpless and defiant. "Fuck it, I'll leave."

"Don't."

"You're not afraid I'll murder you too?"

"Will you?"

"Of course not. I was fucking set up."

"How? What happened?"

"Look man, I don't really want to talk about all that."

"Okay, but maybe talking about it would help." I know I'm treading on very thin ice now. Buddy looks at me, his narrow eyes growing narrower. Then suddenly all the tension seems to drain from his body.

"Yeah," he says in a low voice, "maybe so. I don't know anymore." He starts to speak again, hesitates.

"Go on."

"I don't know man. Shit, you don't really want to hear about it, do you?"

"Yes."

"What happened was I picked up this john in a bar. The man who was killed. I hustle a little on the side, okay? So I left the bar with this john, a real creep, spent the night at his place over in Berkeley. The guy turned out to be a real asshole. The next morning he gave me the runaround, ended up paying me only twenty dollars, which was fifty-five short, you know? But what could I do?"

"At least you got something."

"Yeah, I got something. Trouble. Lots of trouble is what I got. Because the next night this same guy was murdered. Shot through the head in his own fucking house, the place I'd been the night before. Real creepy. Anyway, the cops got onto me because one of this guy's trips was taking pictures, you know?" I know. "And the cops found this picture he'd taken of me at his house. They started showing it around, and some asshole told them that I left the Cat's Meow with the guy, Irving was his name, the night before he was killed. But you see, while all of this was happening, I was in Detroit, working a job. I was staying in this mansion outside of Detroit in Grosse Pointe, which happens to be the richest town in the country, you know? What happened was this john saw my picture in some magazine and got hold of me and arranged for me to fly out there and spend two weeks with him. I left the day after I met Irving. I *knew* I shouldn't go out that night. Karma, you know? And sure enough, when I came back from Detroit to *this* fucking town, I found out that my picture had been in the paper and the cops were looking for me.

"I was scared shitless. Who wouldn't be? I just wanted to run. But I know this john, actually he's a friend of mine, who's a lawyer. So I called him up, and told him what was going on, and he told me to go down and turn myself in right away. So I hauled ass down to the county jail, this lawyer friend of mine went with me. Have you ever been inside the place?" I shake my head no. "It's huge and the coldest place I've ever seen, all glass and marble and *evil*. And the cops started going after me there, my lawyer was telling me when to answer questions and when not to, but it was awful, they questioned me for hours and hours. But you see, it was all bullshit, because the thing is this: I had a fucking alibi. I was in Detroit when Irving was offed, and fortunately the guy I went to see there is no pussy, and when the cops finally agreed to call him—at my fucking expense—he backed me up. Plus there were the airline tickets and the guy's friends that I'd met when I was in Detroit, so you see I could *prove* I wasn't even in town when this guy Irving was offed."

"So the police let you go?"

"They had to. Finally. Pigs didn't have anything on me, couldn't keep me in jail, but I knew the whole thing was going to ruin my reputation in this fucking town. You're not the first person who's remembered that picture in the paper."

"Did they ever find the real killer?" My question seems to surprise Buddy.

"No," he finally says, "I don't think they ever did. Who gives a shit anyway? Fucking john deserved to die, all the trouble he caused me."

"He didn't deserve to die." Buddy gives me a strange look.

"Maybe not," he reluctantly concedes.

We sit silently for a long while in the darkening room, then I get up and switch on a lamp and put a tape of Keith Jarrett on the stereo. Buddy meets me in the center of the room, his brown eyes now innocent, devoid of anger. As we kiss our hands explore each other's bodies, tentatively and tenderly at first, then more passionately. Buddy pulls my T-shirt over my head, asks if I've got any leather.

"You into leather, Buddy?"

"Sometimes," he grins. "And you?"

"Whatever you want. There are some jackets and other stuff in the closet at the end of the hall you'd look good in. Why don't you take a look, put on anything you like. You can pick out something for me too if you want."

"You're a sexy fucker."

"So are you." I watch him saunter down the hall, the flesh of his bare back pale and somehow touchingly vulnerable. Unlike Buddy, I will never tell my story. With luck, we'll both survive.

When I step onto the balcony, the lush perfume of jasmine drifts up to me from the hillside garden, and the entire glittering, magical city stretches out before me, bathed now in the waning deep blue glow of early evening. Already people have turned on lights all over town, signs of life twinkling on the pastel-dotted hills. Downtown several tall glass towers appear to be in flames as they reflect the blood-red rays of the dying sun. Beyond the burning buildings, headlights snake into beautiful, geometric patterns on the bayside freeway before disappearing onto the bridge that leads to the Berkeley hills.

I turn to see Buddy coming toward me in high boots

and my black leather jacket. He steps onto the balcony, touches my shoulder.

"Doesn't look like there'll be any fog tonight," he says.

"Maybe later." As he circles his arms around me, the leather is smooth and cool against my skin.

"You really take care of your body," he says.

"The French call this *l'heure bleue.*"

"What?" Buddy's arms tighten around my chest.

"The time just before nightfall. The color of the sky."

Outstanding Bestsellers!

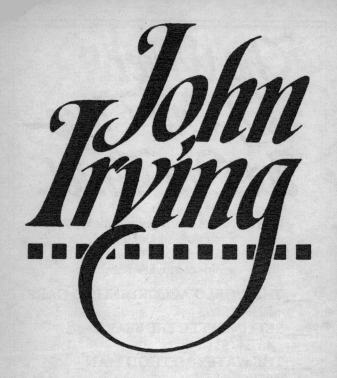

John Irving is the author whose novels
have touched the hearts and minds of millions
of readers of every age.

THE WORLD ACCORDING TO GARP
captured the imagination of millions
and became a phenomenal bestseller.
THE HOTEL NEW HAMPSHIRE became an instant and enormous bestseller.

Irving himself has been the subject of
features in all the media—including
the cover story of *Time*.